THE ALBATROSS AND OTHER STORIES

The Albatross and Other Stories

Susan Hill

First published in Great Britain 1971
by Hamish Hamilton

Published in Large Print 1995 by ISIS Publishing Ltd,
7 Centremead, Osney Mead, Oxford OX2 0ES,
by arrangement with Richard Scott Simon Ltd

British Library Cataloguing in Publication Data
Hill, Susan
Albatross and Other Stories. – New ed
I. Title
823.914 [FS]

ISBN 1-85695-383-1 (hb)
ISBN 1-85695-239-8 (pb)

Printed and bound by Hartnolls Ltd, Bodmin, Cornwall

For Richard Simon

CONTENTS

The Albatross

It was Wednesday. He had gone along the beach as usual for the fish. Nobody else bought fish that way, now, in small, individual pieces, straight from the men, nobody else. He always felt ashamed, trudging very slowly along the great sweep of shingle, the paper for it ready under his arm, he did not want to get there. He saw the men in their little dark huts lined up behind the boats, felt them looking out at him, laughing.

Though they were easy enough with him when he was there, they said nothing as they slit their long knives down the belly of a fish and gouged out the slippery pink innards, looking at the weight of the piece they had given him, guessing a price. And Duncan said nothing to them, had never done so, in all the time he had been coming down here, nothing at all, after he had asked for what he wanted. Only smelled the oil and brine and tar of the huts, and the thick tobacco from their pipes, only shifted his boots upon the wooden floor. He dared not wonder what they really thought of him, or how they talked, as he went away, back towards Tide Street, his heart still thumping, inside him with relief after dread.

At Todd's fish shop in Market Cross, it was different, there were the grained, stained boxes piled up against the wall, from Grimsby and Yarmouth and Hull, there were kippers and mackerel and turbot and pink-spotted plaice, upon the slab.

"You don't go buying any of our fish from that Todd's, thank you, and you go down the beach like I tell you, that's what we've always done, isn't it? I'm not paying good money in aid of Todd's gold-painted signs and fancy new refrigerators." For once, years ago, he was pushing her wheelchair down Market Cross, and there had been a great blue lorry and seven men heaving a new refrigerator into Todd's shop. Later on came the newly-painted sign, swinging in the east wind. She had never forgotten.

So that he must still go, every Wednesday morning, or else in the late afternoon, when he returned from the Big House, down to buy just enough for the two of them, from the fishermen on the beach. It was always Wednesday.

"Not cod," she had told him, over and over again, and written it down with one of the thick, black carpenter's pencils she kept all about the cottage. She underlined the words twice, as he waited.

"NOT COD."

"There's only cod, boy," the man said, Davey Ward this time, the only one of them in the huts, Davey Ward with the scarlet burn down one side of his face, making the skin shine. He had turned and slung the fish guts into the bucket with the rest, rolling the cod up briskly into Duncan's paper. "Nothing much but cod this time of season."

Duncan stood dumbly, alarmed by the huge size of the man, in the tiny hut. He did not know whether one man, looming over him, were as bad, or worse, than all of them together, talking.

Davey Ward delved his thick fingers about in the pockets of his trousers, feeling for change.

Outside it was all but dark, the January sky like slate, and moving with clouds. The beacon flashed green, on-off, on-off, out to sea beyond the breakwater. Duncan walked down nearer to the waterline and then away, face into the wind, listening to the crunch and chop of his rubber boots as they bit into the shingle.

Behind him, Davey Ward raised the bucket and tossed the fish offal into the sea, and the gulls lifted at once off pebbles and water and came down from all the red roof-tops of Heype, gathering overhead, rawking for their food.

"What did I say about it? Just this morning? What did I say?"

Duncan stood helplessly in front of her wheelchair, holding the open parcel in his outstretched hands, looking down at where the cold, flat strips of fish lay, marble-white.

"What did I say?"

And written down, too, as she wrote everything down for him, every message, every demand, every list. Years before he could read himself, the notes had been there, to be handed to other people. He had not read anything until he was ten.

"NOT COD" she had written, and folded the torn-off piece of greaseproof paper into a square and held him to her by the edge of his coat, while she stuffed it into the left-hand pocket.

"Look now, I'm putting it in here, in your pocket on

this side, don't you forget where it is when you get there, just you think on."

He did not need the pieces of paper, the written messages and lists, he had never needed them, he could remember. So that always, when he got out of sight of the cottage, he took them out and tore them up into small pieces and threw them away. For all these years, he had done so, because the notes shamed him, they were things he hated. She used her hands to write them, and so, to carry them in his pocket would have meant that he must carry *her* with him, even when he was away from the house. He would not do that, he did not need the lists. But he no longer tried to make her understand, or believe him.

"You'll have it written down," she said, propelling her wheelchair viciously in and out of doorways, all about the small kitchen. "You don't remember things, you never have, not properly, you need it written down. I'm your mother aren't I, do you think I don't know about it better than you?"

And she was not the only one. Mrs Reddingham-Lee wrote things down for him, if there were more than two jobs she wanted him to do, or any message to be taken, things to be fetched. He worked for Mrs Reddingham-Lee, at the Big House.

"Now Duncan, come here — now, here is your list, I have written it all down, there is nothing for you to do but give it to them, nothing for you to worry about."

She spoke to him in a very clear tone of voice, a little more loudly than she would speak to any other.

"Duncan is perfectly all right," she told her friends,

"he is perfectly reliable, Duncan is not a defective. He is just a little slow, he has not always got everything quite clear in his mind."

She felt, though she would not have said so, that the world owed a little thanks to her, some special grace or other, because she employed the boy Duncan.

But it was not the same with Cragg. Cragg had known him since he was born, eighteen years, and known his mother — Cragg and Mrs Cragg. Though they had nothing to do with them, they were not friends. But alone with the boy, working during the day in the stables and toolsheds, the cellars and the garden and the conservatories of the Big House, Cragg did not give out any written lists, he wasted no breath on repetition. Cragg gave him orders, one, two, three, harsh as bullets. Duncan heard them and remembered, there were no mistakes.

He did not know which way he preferred to be treated — for there had only ever been that simple choice: between the written-down messages and careful speaking of Mrs Reddingham-Lee, and the orders of Cragg. It was one or the other of these ways with everyone who knew him in Heype. And then there was his mother.

"What did I say?"

He wanted to put the fish down, he could smell the sharp, briny smell, filling the back kitchen, and his hands were cold and numb from it, underneath.

"Not cod, I said it twice, more than twice, I wrote it down, didn't I? Didn't I write it down?"

"It's all there was."

He wanted to ask her what else he should have done, whether she would have wanted him to come back with nothing at all, what they would have eaten for supper then, and how could he have asked for the fish and then rejected it when he saw that it was cod, when it had all been done so quickly, taken and slit open, filleted and wrapped by Davey Ward. But he said nothing.

"I hate it, cod. I hate the sight of it, all filled up with water, I told you that."

"It's all they catch just now, it's all there is. In January. It's the bad season,"

"The bad season!" she echoed his tone of voice. "What do you know about that?"

"He told me. He said. There is nothing else, only the cod."

"That's all they want to tell you. You don't know anything about it. Your Mrs Reddingham-Lee doesn't have cod, cod, cod, up at the Big House. No."

"They get their fish at Todd's."

"Well you don't, you go along the beach, always have done. I'm not buying from that Todd."

Hilda Pike's fingers still rubbed up and down the rims of the wheels, he heard her voice saying what it always said to him, over and over again, like the waves turning themselves on to the beach.

"You never listen, that's your trouble, isn't it? You dream. It's no wonder you're like you are, you never try to help yourself, never."

Sometimes, when she began like this, and at other times too, for no reason, he felt a confused anger welling up inside himself, so that, as a small boy, he had gone along through the marshes, beside the river, for hours, beating and beating at the reeds with a stick, or throwing pebbles one after another, hard into the sea. Once, he had kicked his own feet against the school wall until the canvas of his plimsolls split, and his toes were grazed and bruised and bleeding.

Not now, not for a long time. Now, he listened and felt numb. Yet he was more vulnerable, too, as he grew up, even less able to defend himself. But now, he did nothing, only looked after her, pushing the wheelchair up and down the streets, lifting and carrying her, helping her to dress, only learned to cook and clean and do the work they gave him up at the Big House. Only went and stood for hours on end, looking at the sea.

The kitchen had gone quite dark, he could just see his mother's hands, white on the chair wheels, and the steel of her spectacle frames, the metal of a saucepan on the black stove.

"Who was it sold you that?"

"He was the only one there, Davey Ward, he said . . ."

"*Mr* Ward."

"Yes, Mr Ward."

"He's nothing to do with you, he isn't a friend, none of them are. Calling him by his name! They've nothing to do with us at all."

"No."

But Duncan thought suddenly of Ted Flint and his mind filled with pictures, like the tide tumbling into a rock pool. Ted Flint was his own age, Ted Flint, with the dense blue whorls and stripes of tattoo covering his arms and chest, his own boat.

"You go for the fish and you come away again. That's

all. They're not the sort of people you want to get in with, haven't I always told you that? Didn't I tell you from the start, from when you were at school?"

"Yes," he said. "Yes."

"We live our own life, we keep ourselves to ourselves, in this town."

He had wondered, ever since he could remember, why she had come here with him, when he was one month old, why she had settled in this place at all. He knew almost nothing about her, she would not tell him of the past. "We keep ourselves to ourselves in this town."

But he had always lived here, he had gone to school and then left it, and looked after her since the accident, he did not know any other place. He had walked the streets and the paths inland along the river bank beside the flat, still marshes, he had known winter and summer, autumn and spring here, in Heype and nowhere else, he knew every line and fold in the faces of the people, every brick of the cottages opposite their own in Tide Street. He belonged here, even if, lately, he had begun wanting to go away. Yet she talked as if they would not stay here, as if he must not attach himself to anything or anyone. She had chosen to come, chosen it as their place, but for eighteen years, they had lived quite apart from it. Because of the accident, she could never move elsewhere, she was bound to the town and the cottage and to her wheelchair. Nothing was said.

Walking along the sea wall, past the old quay and the martello tower, and then on for miles across the pale stretches of shingle, Duncan thought, she will not let me go, or truly stay, I can neither have this nor that, nothing I want. But he could not sort it out, he had never understood the workings of his mother's mind, nor questioned any of her reasons.

"Well?" she said now, and spun round suddenly in the chair, so that he started backwards, coming up against the edge of the wooden draining board, beside the sink. She had unhooked her stick and reached up with it to switch on the light.

"You'd better cook it, hadn't you? Fry it, cod or whatever it is, there's nothing else to eat."

"No. I asked. I did ask but he said there wasn't anything else. Only the cod!" He was trembling a little, with the effort of trying to explain to her.

His mother looked at him out of the sharp, tight-skinned face, and he saw a momentary softening cross it, like a shadow on the surface of the sea. But it was nothing more than scorn. "You'd believe anything," she said, "do anything they asked you. You've always been like that. Soft. They could tell you anything at all."

He wanted to cry, holding the cold fish, because he had not done right, because he was as he was and could not please her.

But, all that day, there had been the thought of going away, filling his mind. On his own, of going wherever he chose.

It was after Cragg had told him about Southampton. Usually, Cragg told him nothing, did not talk at all, except to give out orders, even if they were doing some job together. Not even over their lunch. In good weather, they sat outside, on the green bench behind the conservatory, where the sun caught their faces, reflected off the glass. The Big House was built on the last of the cliff ledges up above the town, it overlooked all the other roof-tops of Heype, as they went down in layers to the sea. But in winter, there was a coke brazier in the toolshed and they sat on upturned boxes and a broken wicker chair, eating their sandwiches, drinking tea from flasks.

Long ago, Mrs Reddingham-Lee had said, "There is the kitchen, Mr Cragg, goodness me! You have no need to sit in that dark old shed, you should come and be comfortable in the kitchen." And she had offered the services of the daily woman, Mrs Beale, for freshly brewed pots of tea.

Three years ago, when Duncan had come to work here, she had offered yet again. Cragg had said no. "No, thank you very much," for he was a stubborn man, independent, he wanted to eat his sandwiches out of the way of the house and of Mrs Reddingham-Lee. In the shed, he was his own master. He drank from the private flask of tea put up by his wife each morning.

Duncan cut his own sandwiches, prepared his own flask, he had not dared to go against the orders of Cragg, though he would have liked to sit in the warm kitchen, to feel a sense of belonging inside the Big House. They sat and drank and ate for forty-five minutes, summer and winter, between twelve-fifteen and one. It was hot in the toolshed, the brazier glowed red, piled up with coke. Cragg unlaced his boots and loosened them and then read his newspaper from cover to cover, hunched up against the wall, saying nothing. He was a man with a rough-textured, bumpy face, a secret expression.

But today, Duncan had mended the broken hammock.

He had sat just outside the toolshed and knotted patiently in and out with a ball of thick twine, until it had been complete. Cragg had slung and tied it between the two apple trees and climbed up to test the strength. Out of the house, down through the drawing-room windows and across the lawn, came Mrs Reddingham-Lee. "The hammock! Oh, now, Duncan, you *are* clever, how very clever of you! You have mended the hammock, and just when I was so sure we must have a new one, it looked so badly torn and eaten away. How splendid!" and she clapped her hands together and gave the hammock, with Cragg in it, a little push.

"That'll hold," Cragg said. "Yes," and nodded, climbing out and down. He had doubted if the boy would manage it, in spite of his slow patience, so that now, grudgingly, he was pleased, he liked to think of things saved and mended, of a job satisfactorily done.

Which was why he allowed himself to talk, briefly, over their lunch in the toolshed, about a visit to his daughter, married to a docker in Southampton.

"*You've* never seen anything like it, I'll tell you, you never have. The ships. Big as Heype church, easy. Yes, I wouldn't doubt it."

Duncan dared not move, scarcely dared breathe, sitting in the dry, soil-smelling shed, for fear that Cragg might notice his presence and stop talking, go back to his newspaper and deny him any further glimpses into this new, miraculous world.

"You've got the liners, of course, those to America and South Africa and such. Ships you see there, they've been across all the seas of the world."

Duncan tried to picture them and failed, he had only a dim vision of something as big as a church and of the sea stretching away for thousands of pale blue miles. He thought, *I* could go. That's the thing I want to do. I could go. His head was filled with this picture, of the endless sea, and of his own sailing on it, far away.

"Great cranes they have, you see, swinging across with the cargoes, and the luggage. And all the people, rolling up in their smart cars, of course. The passengers." Cragg bit hard into his slab of meat sandwich.

Anxious to show that he had something to contribute to a conversation between them. Duncan said, "I saw the trawlers. At Lowestoft. I've been and seen those." He was stammering.

"Lowestoft!"

Duncan shrank back into himself.

"I'm talking about ships, aren't I? Real ships. *You've* never seen anything like it."

A gust of wind blew the door of the toolshed open suddenly, and there was the winter sky, bleached and grey as a gull's back. Cragg stood up.

"You want to take yourself off, get on a train, you want to go and see them for yourself." For he had not such a low opinion of Duncan's capabilities as others in Heype.

"Southampton?"

"Southampton docks, Portsmouth, anywhere. You never have seen anything like it. They have day trips, down from London."

Duncan screwed the plastic cup back on to the top of his flask and could not make it fit, his hands were trembling. I could go, he thought, I could go anywhere. Even though he had been no further than the port of Lowestoft, outside Heype. I could go.

"I want that bottom bed dug over," Cragg said. "Get out the big fork."

Every now and again, throughout that day, the recollection of it had come back to him, and his heart began to pound with the shock, the impossibility and the excitement of it. It took him a long time, stabbing the big fork into the frost-hardened earth and turning it over, to sort out each separate part of the idea to get it clear in his head. The soil crumbled, sweet-smelling, and he bent down from time to time to pull out woody bits of old root, and fleshy white bulbs, from between the prongs of the fork. It was very cold. Behind him, the wind blew up the hill off the sea. When he rested for a moment, turning round, he could see it there, spreading flatly away, and the river, steel-coloured on the other side, running between the marshes. He would have been happy to work in the garden all the time. A yard away, a thrush pecked into the freshly-turned soil.

Ipswich. Yes. He would get on a bus at the end of Market Street and he would ride on that to Ipswich. It was a fair way, over twenty miles. He had never been. From Ipswich, the trains ran to London, and from London the trains ran everywhere, to any of the places he might choose. Though these were only names in his mind, he could not picture them, nor how he would get about in them, what he would do. He wished, after all, that there were another way, that he could walk down to the beach and get into a boat and go, as the fishermen all went, disappearing over the horizon. Though he knew that, in fact, none of them went far, only four or five miles out, to the sandbank. He had watched them for years, heard them talking about it and then tried to imagine how it would be, putting the boats out, nose facing the open sea. He had never been, never been on the water.

"The sea's not safe," his mother said. "You wouldn't do on the sea, you wouldn't know how to manage, you don't go off in any of those boats. That's a dangerous place."

Then why had they come here, to a cottage in Tide Street? Though perhaps it was because she mistrusted the sea that they did not overlook it. Here, it was small and dark, sheltered behind the tall houses of the seafront.

"You keep away, it isn't any place for you, you leave it alone." As though the sea were some dangerous dog which he must never stroke. But she had been born beside it, he knew that much, in another town, farther up the coast. She had always lived there.

"Nobody could trust you in any boat, muddling about. You stay as you are."

And now, he longed for the sea, watched it and walked beside it, and thought of how it would be, to get away, like the men, in the early morning. He remembered Cragg talking about the liners as big as churches, crossing all the seas of the world. All that. And yet he dared not go too near, when the water ran high and rough in winter, the surf bursting on the shingle in thunder and clouds of spray, he came away from it in dread.

The wind was dropping now, he felt the sweat run down his back, beneath the heavy jumper. There was a long, even line of darker soil, where he had worked his way right across the flower bed. He liked digging, he could do it well, and carefully, there was nothing about it to confuse him. The thrush hopped nearer, on its twig-like legs, and then froze, sensing his own stillness, waiting.

From the house, the voice of Mrs Reddingham-Lee. "Duncan! Now come up here, Duncan, will you, there is something I would like you to get for me, in the village."

At once, he began to be anxious about whether to leave the fork stuck here in the ground, whether he would have time to come back and finish the patch later, or if he ought to take it away now, into the shed, and clean it. Whichever he did, Cragg might tell him that he had been wrong. The day was no longer simple. His shirt stuck to his back, across the thin shoulders.

"Duncan!"

The thrush took off and flew across the garden, into a hedge. In the kitchen of the Big House, Mrs Reddingham-Lee sat down and wrote out a list on a fresh sheet of paper, in large capital letters.

I could go, Duncan thought. It's what Cragg said. *I could go.*

"That wall," said Hilda Pike, "that front wall, it's crumbling down, it's falling to pieces, the plaster's just coming away."

She owned the cottage, she had come to Heype with £900, eighteen years ago, and bought and furnished it, and now it was falling apart, the builders were needed, painters and electricians and plumbers. But there was no longer any money.

"It looks bad," she said, "right on the street. It's a disgrace. That's not how decent people live." For the cottage had always looked neat and tight and well-kept, for the eyes of neighbours, the two small windows up and down carefully curtained, the brick whitewashed and clean. There was a bit of path and a bit of garden and then the gate, and the wall which was coming down. None of the other cottages in Tide Street had any garden, people walked out of their front doors, straight into the road. Theirs was better, Hilda Pike said, theirs was different, though inside it was still poky and cramped, two up two down, and without much light. Down narrow alleys, running in between the houses that faced it, glimpses of the sea.

"You'll have to set it up again. You can get cement, and use what brick there is, you'll have to spend a Saturday and Sunday on that wall, it's a sight."

They had eaten the fish supper, the cod she had not wanted, and he had done the washing up, while his mother dried, sitting close up beside him at the little sink, in her wheelchair.

In the front room, there was a log on the fire. Mrs Reddingham-Lee had sent him home from the Big House with a pile of logs, from the cut-down pear trees, a week before Christmas. Duncan had been terrified, pushing the wheelbarrow down the sloping lanes, for his mother would refuse them, as she refused all the gifts, and offers of help from others, from the neighbours, or people like Mrs Reddingham-Lee. He had worried about what he might do with the logs, where else they would go.

But she had not refused. "*They've* no use for old trees," she had said, unaccountably, "they can afford to throw them out, can they? It's nothing to them, it's only wood. Wood's free."

He had spent every morning for a week, sawing them up into smaller pieces, and then piled them most carefully together, in a single pyramid, outside the back door. He liked to look at them there, he would go and lift one and feel the roughness and the weight between his hands. It upset him, to watch them disintegrate upon the fire.

Every piece of furniture had been in the cottage since the beginning, she had come to Heype with nothing and bought all of it, and no more since, so that he knew the shape and colour and texture of everything, hated it all. Southampton, he thought, ships as big as churches across all the seas of the world! I could go anywhere, do anything. *I could go*. His head sang.

Ted Flint had gone, as soon as he left school, he had gone on the trawlers from Lowestoft, sailing all winter up to Denmark and Iceland, three, four months away at a time. While he was gone, Duncan had thought about him, tried to imagine what jobs he did, what the ship smelled like, the look of the iced-up sea. He had started his own job, at the Big House, what bits and pieces Cragg would trust him with at first — picking up old flower pots and washing the cars. In the streets of Heype, he had seen Ted Flint's mother and wanted to ask her questions, to know about the trawlers. But he dared not. He had been at school with Ted Flint.

When he came back from the trawlers, he was huge,

taller than Davey Ward and coarse-bearded, his arms covered with the blue tattoos. He had bought his own boat, then, and set up, and the others had accepted him at once, because he was a Heype man, he had gone away but still belonged. He was tough now, and often hot-tempered, he would take his boat out in the worst of the gales and seas, when the rest of them did not dare, they stayed behind to watch him and wait, talking about him in the wooden huts. Ted Flint. He was the same age as Duncan, rising nineteen. His father, and his father's father, had both gone down with the Heype lifeboat, a year after he was born. Ted Flint.

Duncan had thought, why did he come back here, *why*? He had seen him on the beach, hauling the boat in over the wooden struts, his hands like raw meat from the cold wind and water. Why? He had gone away and then come back, both of his own choice. Duncan could not understand any of it.

His mother sat with her chair drawn up close to the fire, and her fingers flicked so fast, in and out of the crochet, his eyes could never keep up with them. The white squares and circles of finished work were piling up beside her, on the tall stool. Ever since the accident, she had done nothing else, evening after evening, except the crochet, here, or else sitting out in the tiny back yard, when it was summer. In the Cottage Crafts shop, and Stevens the Draper's, and other shops in towns outside Heype, cushions and shawls and bedcovers made up from all the individual crocheted squares and circles, were expensively for sale. Duncan took the work and brought back the money, sealed in an envelope which he was not allowed to open, and sometimes, he took parcels, the crochet went as far as London, even. He thought about the distance it travelled, from his mother's flicking hands in Tide Street, until it reached the tables and beds and sofas of women like Mrs Reddingham-Lee.

"It's all work for no money," Hilda Pike said, "it's easy enough for them, getting it in, buying and selling, they've not the work, the hours and hours spent. I wouldn't choose to do it."

Once, he had said in tears of misery and desperation, at the sight of the endlessly working fingers, "Don't do it. You don't need to do it. There's what I get, I get money."

He had never forgotten her face, open and bland with scorn, and pity, too, for this boy she had conceived and borne and bred and who was too simple to help himself, or to be trusted, who could not be made to understand.

"*Your* money!"

He knew that she was right, even though they lived plainly enough, that what he brought home from the Big House, and the pension she got because of her accident, was nothing, nothing at all, that the fingers had to go on, flick-flick-flick, in and out of the endless crochet, if they were to live.

Why did we come here? What are we doing here? Where did it all begin? But she would not tell, would not speak to him about his father, or even about her own, about anything to do with the past. Except that, once a year, she had taken him — and now he took her — up the hill to the church, and there, she made him kneel down and pray to God for the eternal rest of his grandmother, who had died on that day. They took a single bunch of flowers, daffodils or anemones, and laid them on some ledge or step inside the church. That was all. She told him nothing about that woman who had been her mother, and so he had no picture in his mind upon which he could focus, it seemed an impossible thing to pray about, a name, a ghost, a shadow. It was March, and the church was always cold. They stayed four or five minutes, only, in silence, and then came home.

Why did we come here?

"Don't you forget. You can do something about it on Saturday, that wall. That'll fall down altogether, otherwise."

The pear log spluttered and then went dead again. They had only one lamp in the front room, up on the table behind her crochet. Everything seemed suddenly dark to him, all the furniture, the dresser and the shiny brown sofa, the stool and the grate and the oak-framed picture of a lake and two mountains. He was stifled, wanting to put out his hands and beat it all away.

"Where are you going? What's all that? Here — what do you think you're off to do, this time of night, Duncan Pike? What . . ."

But he had gone, banging the door and running away from Tide Street, from the cottage and his mother and the broken-down wall.

Outside, it was calm. All afternoon, the wind had been dropping. Now, the sky was clear.

He ran hard for a long way, down Wash Alley and past the coastguard station, out on to the sea defence wall, until he had to stop and catch his breath. The blood was surging in his chest.

It was low water. The sea was flat and scarcely moving. There was a thin moon.

He began to walk, away from the town, on and on, towards the martello tower, looming up through the darkness. The air was raw on his face, beginning to freeze. He had not stopped to put on a jacket or boots, the soles of his shoes made scarcely any noise on the flat concrete slabs of the wall. He would not have walked on the beach, not at night, the crunching of his steps in the shingle would have deadened his hearing of the other night sounds, and he must always be listening, ready for what might come. Since he was a boy, he had grown used to all the sounds of the sea, and to those coming off the river and the marshes, he missed nothing.

He was beyond thinking now, only walked steadily on through the darkness. But feelings gathered inside him, like matter in a wound, and began to press outwards, until he wondered what he might do. He remembered his mother's fingers, working the endless crochet, and the dark little room, the splutter and smell of pear logs on the fire, her voice in his ears.

"*You* don't know. You can't do that. You're not to be trusted with anything. You'd never manage. What have you been able to do?"

And so they all spoke to him, too loudly, as though he were a deaf and dumb boy, they wrote things down for him in lists.

"*You* don't know."

Again, he thought, I can go away, there is nothing I couldn't do. Ted Flint went away. *I could go.*

He stopped, and looked out to where the North Sea lay, stirring beyond him in the darkness. He could go anywhere, by himself.

But he knew why they did not trust him. He was slow, unable to sort things out into clear patterns, to make his way unaided through the maze of decisions and voices and small needs of every day, unable to explain. He was dependent upon his mother, as she was upon him.

At school they had let him draw things, he had held his pencil in a tightly closed fist and never lifted it from the paper, so that all the lines were joined. He drew animals and ships and strangely shaped birds and decorated circles, round and round and round, he was happy doing so, thinking of nothing.

I could go.

The sound of the sea came to him, as it turned over and over on the pebbles, like the wind hissing through summer elm trees. But when he climbed off the wall and slid down the grass bank on to the path beside the river, the swish of the waves receded. Here, it was almost completely still. The water lapped a little up against the mud, and moved secretly in and out between reeds and rushes.

The moon sent long shadows off the martello tower, across the surface of the river. Duncan went closer, his shoes sinking into the rust-tinted mud, so that they made a small suck and hiss. He liked the slippery feel of it through the soles of them, the coldness. Out ahead, in hiding places all over the marshes, the birds would be, dead-still, half-sleeping, the curlews and thin-legged herons and the wild duck.

When he was much younger, they had tried to frighten him with stories about this place at night, about what happened on the river and in the marshes. Smugglers had come up here and been murdered hundreds of years ago and now their ghosts rose up and followed people, phosphor gleamed on the water and false lights and voices led boatmen on to their deaths in the sucking bogs.

He had always been afraid of so many real, definite things, of other people and what they might do, and of the thoughts and feelings within himself. But he was not afraid of these tales that they told him in dark corners, behind the walls of the school, or when they followed him home down the town steps and into the alleys that led towards Tide Street. He could walk out here alone at night and never be afraid. It was different with people, for he could not defend himself against them, there seemed to him no way of predicting what they would do, he dreaded the sight of them, coming towards him, singly or together, their movements and booming voices and the way they might be going to treat him. He could only measure them very slowly, one at a time. Like Cragg. He knew Cragg a little, now, he was not so often startled by the things he said and did. But there were very few others. With the fishermen on the beach, he could never feel safe.

After a long time of standing, listening to the faint sounds, he came away again from the river, up the bank and back on to the wall. The tide was just turning. Looking back, he could see the lights of Heype, glittering up the hill. Then he walked on, he was around the other side of the tower and the emptiness and darkness of the beach and the marshes dropping down. Overhead there was a faint whistling, and then the beating of wings, two or three ducks, flying in from the sea.

He moved again, softly, through the pebbly soil and the sea grass, and into the dry moat running all the way round the tower. The stone walls were huge above him. Everything went dead still, the sound of both sea and river entirely blocked off inside the moat. There was a slab of broken concrete, overturned when they had been making the defence wall. Duncan sat down. He liked the tower. Nobody else seemed to come here now, he could settle behind it and never be seen, he felt protected.

Once, they had kept watch from here, looked out across the sea for the sight of some invading enemy. It was like the keep of a huge castle, the walls of the tower were thick as a man's arm, slabbed and brown-grey. Now, the look-out turret was half broken away, spaces in the stone were thick with climbing bindweed. There was a door at the bottom, you could climb up and get inside. Now, it swung away from its hinges, and beyond that, it was black. He had never gone in there. The others had. When he was at school, he had come and stood on the beach by himself and watched them, they had raced and leaped along the sea wall, and then gone swarming in, exploring cellars and all the rooms up the spiral staircase, until they reached the top and peered out of the turret. It was a dangerous place, crumbling down, private, forbidden. Everyone else had been into it. But he had never gone anywhere with any of them. They had pointed down at him, far below, and called out, waved their hands and shrieked with laughter, their voices carrying on the wind towards him and beyond, echoing far out to sea.

But none of them would dare to come here at night, not even now. When the tides ran high, the water flooded the cellars of the martello. At the beginning they had been used as dungeons, people said, men had been locked in there and left to drown.

The moon shone directly through the open door at the top of the steps, so that he could see more than blackness, he could see a couple of steps, and then shadows a little way inside. Down here, it was quite sheltered, only his face was still cold, though a white frost was beginning to glisten thinly in between the grasses. All around him, there were bits of rock, and stone, twisted bolts of iron and old glass shaped smoothly into pebbles. He thought of what things he might find, hidden in the moat.

Once, walking on the beach near to the lifeboat, he had found a coin, coppery-looking and with some strange markings on it. The edges were quite smooth. He had been anxious about what to do with it, and in the end, had given it to one of the fishermen. The man had half-turned from mending his sprat nets, and slipped the coin in his pocket, nodding to Duncan, saying nothing.

His mother had screamed at him in fury, she made him return to the beach, told him that he must ask for the coin back. But he had not dared. He had walked to and fro endlessly in front of the boats, watching the man continue with his work on the nets, and seen the other men, too, he had heard them laughing and turned his face towards the sea. But he could not have gone near to the man with the coin again.

"I don't know," he said, "I didn't see him. I don't know which man he was."

Her eyes had glittered with disbelief.

"That coin, that might be worth a hundred pounds, more, that might have been anything. *You*! You can't be expected to know, you don't do any good for anybody. You find something on the beach next time and you bring it home here with you, don't you? Here to me. You remember."

But he had never found anything again. Only the curiously shaped pebbles and bits of dry, hollowed-out driftwood, which he took home because he liked them and which his mother threw away. What she must have was the cottage tidy, carefully polished, orderly, the clearance of all bits and pieces.

Now, because he remembered how he had run out of the house so abruptly, giving no reason, thinking nothing of her, he felt a surge of pride and delight, he felt powerful, as though he were suddenly a man like Ted Flint, he could do anything. Though he did not forget the sound of her voice, calling him back, rising higher in anger and fear. For she was afraid to be left alone at night now, she kept her stick hooked over the back of the chair. Without him there, she was helpless, except to propel herself about between front room and kitchen. Besides, she did not trust him, nor believe that he was safe to be out on his own alone.

Something scuttled ahead of him along the tower, and then up the bank, through the sand and grasses. The tower was full of small animals, mice and rats and all the nesting birds. He liked them, any of them, he tried to find live things to hold between his hands.

Above his head, the stars were thick as apple blossom. He began to feel the cold, right through his body.

When he got up, he walked softly around the moat, past the gaping door and returned, to stand on the wall. The air was cold as steel coming off the sea.

"Duncan Pike!" The voice was no more than a whisper, below him on the dark beach.

"Duncan Pike!"

He neither moved nor spoke, he did nothing except wait. His limbs and all the nerves and muscles through his body felt loose and slack, his mind was brimming full, but stopped in its course like the river, overtaken by frost and ice. This was how it was with him, in fear, this or else violent confusion, which sent him pelting away. No single thought or feeling could be separated from the whole, coagulated mass.

"Duncan Pike!"

There was a scrabbling noise, a trundling and dragging of the shingle, and then the clang of metal, a bump, bump, bump, and someone breathing hard, straining with effort.

Two or three yards away from him, a figure emerged up the broad steps in the sea wall, pulling something up behind it. On the shoreline, a wave broke, creaming over softly and then rasping up the sand and pebbles. Silence. The figure began to back a little, closer to him, along the wall. He had not moved but now he knew who it was and his mind loosened a little, enough for him to recognize that he need not be afraid.

She reached his side and stopped. His shoulders were hunched up into his neck, in a defensive gesture, he was thin and slight as a twelve-year-old, in the dark sweater.

"Well now!"

He could feel her looking at him closely, her small eyes searching him up and down. Old Beattie. He had not seen her for a week or two. Out on the sandbanks, the emerald flash-flashed, and then was dark again.

She was friendly towards him, he thought that was now certain. Though very few people in the town trusted her and she lived, Hilda Pike said, like a vulture, off the droppings of others. Every morning and evening she went along the beach, close to the shore, walking for miles, pushing the old pram, her head bent, eyes searching the ground. From time to time she parked the pram, and went to crouch, or even to kneel down, raking her fingers about through the pebbles and taking up this or that to throw into it. There were always stories going about that she knew where to find amber, great lumps of it, somewhere out beyond Thereford Point, that Old Beattie was rich, going off with the stones to Ipswich and bringing back wads of notes to line the mattress of her bed. Others laughed, and said that she found rubbish, nothing, old plimsolls lost by children in the summer sea, and tin cans and wood for kindling. And if she was lucky, a penny or a sixpence. She was poor, they said, Beattie Thorpe had nothing but a pension. But nobody knew, not for certain, she was spied upon and guessed about and never completely trusted.

"Duncan Pike."

"Yes," he said in the end, stammering partly from the cold. And then, "It's weeks. It's a long time. I've not seen you."

She was still looking at him sideways on. What she wore was always the same, the old, bruise-coloured raincoat, long to her ankles, and seeming to billow out curiously, to be padded in odd places.

"Newspaper," she had told him once, "you tie it round yourself, underneath a woollen. Keeps out all the cold, that does."

In the pram there were always newspapers, piled neatly, she collected them every so often from the back doors of houses. She went along the beach, and through the streets of Heype, untroubled by the worst of the weather, in gale and rain and sleet, her head was always uncovered. She wore the same pair of rubber boots, short and very wide at the tops, and faded by salt and sea to a faint coral pink.

Duncan turned his head to look at her, and she seemed to have changed, the red-veined cheeks were slacker over her bones, there was something old and stained about the skin around her eyes. Since he could remember, she had looked the same. She had come to Heype first when he was at the infant school, a boy who was soft in the head, five or six years old. One day she was not known, and the next she was there, pushing the old pram for the first time along the beach. Old Beattie. Her cottage was half-way up the narrow lane leading to Church

Steps, and they had all pelted past it, coming down from school, some of them slung tiny pebbles as they went by, hoping to hit her door or a window. Duncan had come afterwards, trailing behind them on his own. Beattie Thorpe had watched him.

"I know where she comes from," his mother had said once, startling him. "I remember her. You can't tell me about it. Don't you go talking to her."

Occasionally, the two women had passed each other in the street and Duncan had waited, watching them both, aware of some recognition that flickered between them, though nothing was ever said. Old Beattie's eyes had narrowed. His mother had pulled him along.

"She was a funny one, then. She went her own way, went off, and that was that, we none of us saw her again. My mother knew Beattie Thorpe. Yes. But it's time enough ago. It's all past history."

He could not discover more, and dared not ask, her words were like fragments of some other language.

When he was eleven or twelve, Old Beattie had saved his life. It was the beginning of December, early dark, with a thudding sky, the lights were on all the way down the town, as they came out of school. It was a Wednesday. He had to go and get the fish.

There were no men at all in the huts, the seas had been too high, nobody had gone out that day. Duncan had walked, with anxiety mounting in him, from end to end of the row, time and again, going up to knock on the wooden doors, peering desperately into the small windows, expecting some miracle to occur, fish to be had from somewhere. The money for it was wrapped up inside greaseproof paper, and written on the paper was the note. It was the winter after his mother's accident.

The beach had darkened completely and the tide was high, crashing and foaming about the wooden stakes. He had almost cried, not knowing what she was going to say to him, or whether he should go to Todd's shop and buy the fish for supper there, or else to the grocer and ask them what he could take home, for the money she had given him. But it was Wednesday, it was fish day, always, that was the way everything was planned and he was just learning about it, he dared not tamper now with the structure of their routine.

The wind had come roaring across the water, sending a sheet of spray slapping up into his face, blinding him.

When he opened his eyes again, they had been there. Four of them, and bigger than he was. He knew them all, knew their names and faces.

"Dafty! Dafty-Duncan!"

One of them had been Ted Flint.

The salt water was drying on his face in the wind, leaving the skin rough and sore, but his hair was still damp, hanging down coldly on his forehead. All of the huts were dark, there was nobody else at all on the beach. Duncan had stood, waiting for them. He was light enough, and did not resist. They tipped him over and caught him before he fell backwards on to the shingle, but they did not hurt him, as he expected, it was only their white faces that threatened him, their eyes glinting in the darkness. He remembered, now, how he had felt. It had been simply nothing, complete blankness, he might have been dead, he was so afraid.

"Dafty-Duncan; Dafty-dafty-Duncan!" But they had sung in a chorus of whispers, their voices carried away to sea, no risk of being heard by anyone in the streets behind.

"Dafty-Duncan!"

They had spread out one of the mackerel nets and rolled him tightly in it, over and over, until he was a huge bundle. The nets smelled chokingly, of fish and oil and brine and tar, he could scarcely breath. Then they had lifted him up and laid him in the bottom of one of the boats. After that, he heard their footsteps, running away over the stones and up on to the wall, thump-thump, thump-thump, and then gone. A single shout had come back to him through the darkness. After that, nothing. He was cramped, with the cold and the tightness of the hard, knotted net around him, and the bottom of the boat was wet, it came straight through his clothes.

After a moment he had opened his eyes. Humps of cloud moving fast one close behind the other, in front of the moon. The waves crashed over, like cannons booming up the beach.

The water would not reach this far unless a storm got up, the boats were always pulled high, close to the sea wall. But it had never occurred to him that he would do anything but die, he had lain rigid, arms pressing into his sides, the flesh of his hands bitten into by the mesh of the net, waiting. He had not cried out or spoken. The wind was howling.

Old Beattie had got him out. He never discovered how she had known where to find him, whether she had been somewhere down the beach and heard the noise. But, one moment there had been wind and sea and darkness, and then footsteps and the bump of the old pram, and her voice, shouting to him. He had not answered, only lay, she had come down all of the boats until she found him. Then she had climbed up and inside, he had watched the pale-pink rubber boots come over the edge. She had begun to unroll the nets. It took a long time. She looked into his face every so often, murmured something he could not catch, and when he was free of the net she had sat him up and chafed his hands between her own, and put them up to his raw face. She had taken him back to Tide Street, pushing him in the pram, among all the flotsam, the old newspapers. But when they got there, she would not wait, she was half-way back down the street by the time his mother had reached the door.

All over his body, the press of the nets had marked him in odd triangular patterns, so that he could not hide anything of what had happened from her, it had all come stammering out, scarcely coherent.

"Old Beattie," he said, at the end, "she came. Old Beattie."

His mother had been strange towards him, at the same time angry and blaming and oddly tender. In the morning, she had waited for him to come into her bedroom to help her get up. Then she had said, "You needn't start looking about for that old woman, that Beattie, and listening to any of her tales. You've cause to be grateful, and nothing more. She's funny, that one. She means nothing to you."

But from time to time, ever since, he had disobeyed

his mother, and walked some way along the beach with Beattie Thorpe, watching her eyes light upon something that glinted or obtruded from the pebbles, so that she stopped and darted down upon it like a jackdaw, and put it into the old pram. He had grown up and left school and gone to work at the Big House, and he still talked with her now and again. She had said to him, "You know what's what, Duncan Pike, you're all right. You take no notice of what they say to you." In the town, people had said that like called to like.

She never sought out his company, months went by without their meeting or stopping for one another, and he thought that was what she wanted, she was content to be on her own, trundling the old pram.

"I went away," she said now. Her eyes were turquoise. "They had me over at Ipswich, had me in the hospital. I've been away ill."

He stared anxiously at her again, and she could see it, he was alarmed. She screwed her face up suddenly like a monkey, in an expression of self-derision.

"That's all done with," she said, "that's nothing. And what about Duncan Pike?"

"I'm all right."

"You are?"

He waited. The water turned and turned.

"I could go away," he said suddenly, and caught his breath, to hear the words spoken out loud.

Beattie Thorpe was still.

"To sea. Anywhere. I could."

"And would you?"

He felt the words surging up inside him, and tried to

choose the right ones, and not to stutter and stammer, because he needed to explain everything to her, about Cragg and the ships at Southampton and about the other thoughts he had had, way back, about how it had all begun. He wanted to bring Ted Flint into it, too, for he had always meant her to understand that the past made no difference, now, Ted Flint had been one of the boys who left him tied up in the boat, but that was done with, none of it mattered.

He could only say, "I might do anything."

"Well then. You make up your own mind, Duncan Pike, you think about it and do as you choose. Are you listening?"

He shook his head slowly, the confusion was now so great.

"There's not many things you couldn't do, given you set yourself to it."

But he was looking over her shoulder, back towards the lights of Heype, his face suddenly tight with worry. Beattie pulled up the collar of her old mac and shifted about inside the layer of newspapers, preparing to go.

"Yes," she said, expressionlessly. "There's all that."

For she had seen how the boy's mother was with him. She knew Hilda Pike.

"I'll help you," he said now, "with the pram. I'll push it for you."

She let him, watched the careful way he walked ahead of her along the wall, pushing the old pram as he might push a child, or his mother in her wheelchair. He had very long, bony hands, he could do anything with them.

On the corner of Tide Street, she left him, trundling

off with the raincoat flapping about her ankles. Duncan stood watching. Down one of the cuts between the tall houses, he heard the sea. I could go, he thought, I could go now, there are boats on the beach. I could take one. Frost glistened on the surface of the cobbles.

His mother would not speak to him. He asked her questions. "Do you want your milk drink yet? Have I to bank the fire? Is your bottle too hot?"

No reply. She scarcely looked at him. He felt weak with guilt and anxiety, he would have done anything at all to have her say something. It was vital to him to be back in her favour.

He went into the kitchen. It smelled of cold fat and frost on the stone floor, the damp wood of the draining board. He put the kettle on the black stove and waited for it to boil, he pulled back the rug and lifted her out of her chair and carried her upstairs, he laid her on the bed and helped her to undress, he drew the yellow curtains. Everything as usual, everything in the same order.

She was getting even thinner now, and her legs dangled uselessly like doll's legs, when he lifted her from the chair. She was very well, Doctor Nott said so, there was nothing whatsoever the matter with her, she ate well, and slept, though now it was with the help of tablets, she was strong, she might live for ever. It was only that she could not move her legs.

The pear log had gone out, one end almost burned away, charred and powdering, but the other end untouched, hard and green. Underneath, the fire was dead. It was very cold in the front room when he came in. She had not been able to lean down far enough to mend the fire, only to poke about in it with her stick.

"I went out," he said, "I only went out. I needed to walk a bit. I do, don't I? You know. There's nothing wrong in it, I only went out."

She sat motionless in the wheelchair.

"You wouldn't have liked to go. It's cold. It's freezing now, there's all ice in the puddles."

The clock struck half past ten. He had been gone a long time, then, much longer than he had meant. He had no sense of time, walking by the sea. "There's that wall," he went on, "I heard you about the wall, I haven't forgotten, you needn't think. I could start it tomorrow. In the afternoon I could. I've to come home early, Cragg said. He wants me for Saturday, that's why. So tomorrow I'll do the wall, won't I?"

He talked to her that way, on and on, filled with dread by her silence, as he carried her up the stairs, got the things she needed, moved nervously about. When she was lying there, under the sheets and blankets, he stood for a moment, looking down. Her hair was thick and dry and flint-grey, scraped back tightly from her forehead in the daytime, and held with a metal comb. Now, she had loosened it and it waved slightly about her face, softening the line of bone and making her look younger. But she was not young, he thought that she could never have been young. He knew nothing about her.

As a child, he had always told her everything, had needed to make endless confessions. The urge to do so welled up in him now, he wanted to go and kneel down beside her bed, and say, I thought I could go away, I wanted to go away and I went out to the tower, I talked to Old Beattie, I wish I were like Ted Flint, *he* went away, and he came back. *Why*? I could go away.

He said nothing. She turned her face away from him, on the pillow.

"That's everything," Duncan said. "You've all you want now, haven't you?"

He waited for a second, and then walked out of the room. He knew that she had moved her head again, to watch him, and he felt pride, because he had not told her. He had kept something back, and now, he would go on doing it. Everything was changing. "There's not many things you couldn't do," Beattie had said.

Downstairs, he went into the kitchen and brewed himself tea, and then sat in front of the dead fire, holding the china mug between his hands tightly, wide awake with excitement.

Though, in the morning, he could not remember it, and his mother still did not speak to him.

By twelve o'clock, he had finished digging over the old flower-bed and raking the soil finely, it was ready for planting. Cragg came down and looked it over, but he only nodded, surly, the talk about Southampton forgotten. A wind was getting up again, after the previous night's calm, a sharp wind, coming in quick gusts and making the sea choppy and flecked with white, running fast.

Duncan left the Big House and went down to Whick's Builders, to buy cement and sand and whitewash for the wall.

His mother had sat and eaten her breakfast and then

written the note, handing it over to him without a word and watching until he had put it away in his pocket. He had taken it up to the Big House, and burned it in Cragg's bonfire, behind the compost, stirring the ashes over with his foot to make them disintegrate.

"That's heavy now, young Duncan Pike, that weighs half a ton, cement, you'll not carry it."

But he had forced himself to lift and settle it on his back, though he was bent almost double, going out of the builder's yard, the bones of his neck and spine were aching and burning. He could not see or hear the men behind him, only guess at what they said. It was important to do as they did, to manage an impossibly heavy load, without difficulty.

"That'll drop off."

"He's not so daft, that one," Whick said, "he'll do."

"What?" John Dent shook his head and went back to loading grey roof slates on to the truck, his eyes wide with disbelief. Dafty-Duncan! Since he was a boy, he had heard his mother and his aunt talking to him very loudly, when he came into the shop, putting the loaf of bread under his arm and guiding him like a blind person, out of the door.

"Carry it carefully, hold it tight, Duncan. Go straight home, now."

"What do you shout at him for? He's not deaf."

His mother had shrugged, unloading a fresh tray of bread. "He's not the same as you, you've got to make allowances. You have to be sure he understands you, that's all."

And now, today, he had come stammering into the

yard and stood about, his hands and arms never still, eyes huge in the pale, bony face, buying sand and cement and stubbornly heaving it home.

John Dent grinned, piling up the slates, remembering how they had been as kids, the things they had said and done to Dafty-Duncan.

When he reached the cottage and dropped the sack on to the garden, he could scarcely stand upright again, his muscles were like pulled ropes. He did not go inside. She was in the front room, waiting, he could see the shape of her through the net curtains. He turned and walked deliberately away along Tide Street and down one of the alleys.

As he passed by the side of the Ship, the door swung open and shut behind Ted Flint.

Duncan stopped dead. Ted Flint came easily towards him, head cocked back, ears very red, just below the rim of his woollen hat. Bits of blond hair fronded out and over the collar of his jersey. Ted Flint. Duncan could see the tattoos, a rose, an anchor, a bird, a linked pair of hearts, up his thick forearms. He began to move away, towards the lifeboat.

"Well then?" Ted Flint said. Duncan could feel him coming up behind him, head and shoulders taller.

"All right are you, Duncan Pike?"

Duncan stiffened.

"Hey?"

"Yes," he said quickly. "Yes. All right."

For some reason, Ted Flint laughed. He was looking at Duncan. But it was not a vicious laugh, there was nothing behind it. Duncan thought, I could be like him, that's how I ought to be. Ted Flint was everything. Sometimes he spoke, sometimes half-nodded. Often, nothing. But today, he kept pace with Duncan, going across the shingle towards his boat. Sky and sea and beach were all the same colour, merging together and oddly pearled. The breeze had freshened, raising a swell.

They reached the blue and white boat. Duncan thought, this is all I want, I want to stay here. The rest of the men were still at their dinners, or else further off, in the last of the huts.

Ted Flint walked off to the water's edge and stood, gazing down, then lifted his head to measure the waves, tracing them back. The wind was south-east, rolling the sea slantways on to the beach.

Duncan thought of nothing, not his aching back or his mother waiting for him to go home and start on the broken wall, nothing. He would stay here for as long as Ted Flint would let him, content with anything. It was a long time, now, since he had so much as spoken.

Ted Flint wandered back up to the boat, hands in his pockets. He looked like all the others, now, Duncan saw, younger, but old, too, broad and slow and careful, easy-going or evil-tempered, whichever he chose. He looked at Duncan, and his blunt features were luminous with some secret amusement.

"Want to come out in the boat then, Duncan Pike?"

Out. Out in the boat. He was taking the boat out, he would let him come. Duncan could not begin to speak or to think clearly, it was scarcely believable, what Ted Flint had said. "Want to come out?" Out. In the boat.

He would climb in and sit there and they would go, take the nets four or five miles, and then fish along the sandbank, they would disappear on to the sea. He had never been.

Ted Flint paused for a second and then turned and began to get ready, hailing to one of the other men to help him, taking the rust-stained fishing hooks up from where they lay on the beach, and the lines, and luminous orange floats, loosening the cable. Without warning, he began to give Duncan orders, as Cragg did: do this, move that, lift it, let it go, hold it, and Duncan obeyed, transfixed, desperate to please. The other man left them, to walk slowly beside the waterline, smoking his pipe.

The boat was down and ready, the motor running. Ted Flint was standing up in it, towering above Duncan, tall as a king.

"Get in then, if you're coming."

Why should he take me out there, Duncan thought. *Why*? I've never been, I don't know anything, he doesn't speak to me, why should he ask me to go? Though he could sense no animosity in Ted Flint, no threat of danger. He was entirely puzzled.

A wave gathered, battleship-grey and seething along its crest, and then crashed over. The boat lifted and rocked.

"Hey?"

There was a moment when Duncan was ready to spring forwards and up, when he could already feel himself going out to sea, imagine the movement of it beneath him, they were pushing ahead. "Want to come out in the boat then?" With Ted Flint. *I could go.*

And then another wave began to gather, and suddenly, he saw them coming at him, one after the next, rising up higher and higher, ready to break about his head and drag him down into them, and he knew that once they had pushed the boat out, then there would be no escape for him, he would be alone with Ted Flint, towering above him, in the middle of the endless sky and heaving sea, and he was seized with choking panic, he turned and began to run, pounding off down the beach to get away from the menace of the waves and wind, and the chugging of the boat, out of the reach of Ted Flint, he would have done anything rather than go on that sea.

"That's not safe, you'd never manage, you'd not know what to do. You leave going in boats alone."

He reached the steps and scrambled up and raced over the square, making for the dark, close safety of Wash Alley. Later, he would think of the folly of it, and want to claw at himself in helpless anger, later, he would ask again and again what Ted Flint had thought and said, know that there would never in his life be a second chance. He had not dared to go out in a boat, he had been overcome with terror at the sight of the sea, he had run away. So what they said about him was true.

Now, he only wanted to be home, he threw himself in through the door of the cottage and stood in the front room, beside the high oak dresser, panting and shaking, his breath and blood pushing like waves against the thin walls of his chest.

His mother still sat, in the wheelchair, close beside the window, looking out. After a moment she said, "*Now* what have they been doing to you? Now what?"

Duncan leaned his arms upon the dresser and wept, because he had escaped from the sea, and was sick with shame at himself, and because his mother had spoken to him.

All afternoon, he rebuilt the wall. The old mortar crumbled away in his hands, and when he knocked it off the individual bricks, it blew up into his face with the powder of the white-wash, making his eyes smart. He worked very slowly. Cragg had taught him how to do a job. The whole wall had to be pulled down, to the bottom layer of brick, it would take far longer than this one afternoon, perhaps even longer than the weekend.

When he bent his back, the muscles hurt between his shoulders. From the window, behind the net curtains, his mother watched him.

After his fit of crying had stopped, he had not answered her question, he had said nothing at all about what had happened. It had become, within a few days, the most important thing with him, not to do so, never to tell her anything again.

She had followed him into the back kitchen.

"What have they done to you? Who was it? What have they said?"

He began to take eggs out of the wicker basket on the table but she had driven the chair hard across the kitchen towards him, slapping down his hands. "You leave that to me, I'll do that. You're not in any state, not for anything, look at you."

Duncan pushed his hands deep inside his pockets to

stop the trembling. His mother set the bowl on her lap and broke the eggs into it and began to beat them.

"I don't know what's happened to you, Duncan Pike, I don't. Something's happening. You mind what you're about, these days. You're not a baby now, are you? You'll go the way they all said you'd go, you'll just play into their hands, won't you? Losing your temper, crashing out of the house, crashing in again, fits and tantrums. You try and keep a hold on yourself. You're not a baby, you've to learn things. You mind what you're about."

He wanted to ask her what she expected of him, for in the past it had always seemed to be so little, she had told him over and over again the things he could not, would never be able, to do, had told him that he could not expect life to treat him as it treated others. Expect nothing from yourself.

Now, he was groping towards all the new possibilities, they shimmered just ahead, he could see them, and hear them inside his own head, he wanted everything. But she told him to mind himself, to be careful, told him he would not manage, and at the same time, that it was the other people, they were the ones who shook their heads and expected nothing of him. He was behaving now, as they had all waited for him to behave.

But it's *you*, Duncan said, it is you, it is you, you, and struck the trowel hard down the edge of a brick, so that it went on, into his hand. The knuckles, already sore and stiff with cold, spouted little beads of blood in a long line. He scarcely hesitated and did not look up, for she must not see what had happened, he would not do anything about it. It was his own fault.

When he was almost five, she had taken him, once only, and for some unspoken reason of her own, up to the swings in the small children's playground at the top of the town. Nobody else had been there.

"Push," she had told him. "Push with your legs. You don't need me to do everything for you, there's something you can do for yourself. *Push*."

Very awkwardly, he had learned how to bend his knees back and then forwards again, to the rhythm of the swing, until he began to go higher, without meaning it, too high, the sky had lurched about and he had been filled with dread.

"Get off now," he said, and the swing had rocked a little, he was sitting at an angle on the wooden plank, unbalancing it. "Off now, off." He was still unable to talk clearly, only she could understand him. "Off, now."

She had done nothing, only stood, as though wanting him to fall, or as though she might be unaware of him, were thinking of something else, in some other place. She was wearing the bottle-green coat with the beige fur collar, the same coat she had always worn.

He had screamed, to try and bring her back to this place. "Off now, get off, get off, *get off* . . ."

In his agitation he had fallen, not far or badly, only the palms of his hands were grazed, but he had seen the black ground coming up to meet him, had felt the bump and the jarring and expected all the bones to come pushing out in every direction, through his own flesh, he had screamed with the shock of it.

She had waited, had not picked him up or spoken to him, only stood, staring blankly ahead of her and kneading her fingers inside her coat pockets, until he got himself up.

"All that screaming!" she said at last, pulling him away by the hand. "All that. You're not hurt, that was nothing. They don't want that when they have you at the school, I'll tell you. That screaming. No. We won't come here again, will we?"

And they had not, to Duncan's relief, swinging had been one more thing that he could not do. It seemed to him that she had one of her lists hidden somewhere about her, to which she added, each day, his new failures. There were trials set for him and he did not pass. When he hurt himself, she was cold towards him, sometimes getting plaster or ointment or disinfectant out, but angrily, as though he were to blame. Yet he remembered a fever, once, when he had lain in bed with terrible nightmares, clinging like bats to the inside walls of his head, and then he had woken to find her sitting on the painted wooden chair, close up to his pillow, her face full of anxiety, holding his hand. He had been more than ever bewildered, wondering why he should suddenly merit her kindness. Later, he had thought about it carefully, and seen that he was to blame only for accidents, for the cuts and bruises that came with bumps or falls.

After that, he went in trepidation about the world, holding himself in, avoiding every conceivable object of danger. He watched the others riding bicycles in Market Street and swarming up the martello tower, and wading out into the middle of one of the streams, looking for fish, and he caught his breath for them, terrified by their physical ease and struck dumb by the pressure of his need to warn them, warn them. Your own fault, he would have said, listen, listen, it will be your own fault, you will be to blame, nobody will help you.

Then, a boy had fallen from some railings in the school yard, upside down on to his head, and that had been his own fault, that was an accident, the ambulance had come and taken him to hospital and he had been there for three weeks. But they had all been told to write the boy letters, they had brought gifts for him and made up a class story, and Duncan must do drawings, because he could not write. Once again, he was thrown into confusion. A boy had fallen, he had been to blame, and yet the teacher, Miss Napp, said, "Everyone must think of something specially nice for Malcolm, poor Malcolm, everyone must be kind to him."

In silence, Duncan had drawn his drawing and shut his mind off from the impossible question, his pencil moving round and round and round.

So that, when he cut the blade of the trowel across his cold knuckles, he shook the blood off and then pressed his hand briefly against his coat. That was all, for he was to blame, he would say nothing.

All afternoon, he thought of Ted Flint, out fishing in the blue and white boat. He could hear the sea tossing about, at the end of Wash Alley. His own fear of it had been a shock to him, for he had never seen the waves in such a light before, he had liked them, walked by them, he had wanted the sea to take him away. He could swim, it was not that, for they had all gone to the small pool up by the tennis courts, when he was in Class V, and he had not found it difficult, after a while, to push his limbs out across the water, he had never thought to be frightened.

"You listen, Duncan Pike. You don't go swimming in that river, and you don't go in the sea. Never mind the others, they're different, they've nothing to do with you. It's not safe, you wouldn't manage. You go in the water at the pool when they take you, and that's all."

But he had never thought of disobeying her, for the others went down to swim in the river all together and they did not offer to take Duncan.

He stirred the cement about and then ladled it thickly on to the flat brick. Ted Flint, he thought, Ted Flint. I could have gone.

When he could bear it no longer, he put the trowel down on the wall and went, he had to see whether the boat was back.

At first, there was nothing, as far as he could see on the heaving, steely water. A fine rain had started, blowing into his face from off the sea. He stood by one of the stakes, screwing his eyes up to look ahead. Then, out of nowhere, the boat appeared, coming in fast towards the shore and pitching, like a train on a switchback. Ted Flint was standing up, his bright yellow oilskin like a beacon against the sky.

Down at the water's edge, Davey Ward stood, waving his arms up and down to guide the boat in. It would have been all right, Duncan thought, he's here, he has come back. It would. I could have gone. He wanted to cry, and he wanted to go and hide in the alleys, out of sight of Ted Flint's eyes, the jeers of the other men. But he did not move, he stayed, looking on, needing to be by the sea.

The boat came in on the swell of a wave, and there was the scrape of the wood grazing to a halt on sand and shingle. Duncan saw the water streaming down off Ted Flint's oilskins. His bare hands were purple as plums, laying down the planks to guide the boat up. Someone shouted from the huts and he shouted back, but the words were lost on the wind. Duncan thought, they are friends, they help him, men shouting like that to one another, asking questions and answering, knowing the right things to say. I could have gone, they would have been shouting down to me.

He pictured the inside of the huts, and himself, standing there, and drinking tea and rum, his own red hands around the steaming mug, being one of the others. There was nothing else he wanted.

The cut from the trowel throbbed across his bare knuckles. It was raining harder, his mother would be wanting tea. He thought suddenly of how much he left her alone. But he would have changed that, some way, if he could, and she had never let him. "Mrs Ward might come," he had told her, in the weeks after her accident, "Mrs Napp sent this . . . Mrs Carr asked . . . Old Beattie would push you out . . . Mrs Ward might come . . ."

But she would have none of them. Send them away, don't answer the door, don't take it, no, no, we don't need them, we can manage. And she had taught him to manage, the house and caring for her, and then his job at the Big House, after he left school.

"Blood's thicker than water . . . We keep ourselves

to ourselves in this town . . . You're not my son for nothing Duncan Pike."

Besides, he was too young, and simple, she said, if anyone came and sat with her in his place, what good would that do, where would he go? "I bore you, I bred you, you'd not have managed anything, without me."

So he should go back to her now. He wondered what things went on inside his mother's head, as she sat all day in her wheelchair, doing the white crochet. He did not know what comparison there might be with others, or with himself, and his own muddled thoughts and feelings, as he mended a hammock or dug over the Big House garden, he did not know anything about any other people.

He should go back now. There was a fine cobweb of raindrops over his jersey, clinging to the hairs on the surface of the wool.

"You're a case, Duncan Pike! Daft beggar!"

Ted Flint had come out of the hut again, and down the beach towards him.

"You!"

But he spoke mildly enough. "That's only a bit choppy," he said now, looking at the sea. "Nothing to hurt you."

Duncan looked up, rubbing his fingers anxiously about on the wooden stake. Ted Flint's expression was strange to him, sharp and mocking, but at the same time friendly, genial, as though none of it mattered.

"You'd be all right on the boat, you'd do, give yourself half a chance. I'd shape you."

He said nothing.

"That's getting up now, though." The sky was darkening.

"Want a fish for your tea then, our Duncan?"

His eyes were wide open, glinting with amusement. Duncan felt wary, remembering. But it was Ted Flint.

"It's not . . . I can't. No. Wednesday's fish day, we buy our fish on Wednesdays."

"Not *buy*. I asked you if you wanted a fish, not buy it. I'm giving you one, aren't I?"

He walked off, back into the hut, and came out again a moment later, standing on the step and holding out a package. "Hey up, then!" Duncan hesitated, then made his way very slowly across the shingle. In two of the other huts, he could see lights on, the shadows of the men, knew that they watched him.

"Herring that is, make you grow up a big lad."

After a moment, Duncan took the parcel. The paper was wet already from the fish inside.

"Come out and catch it yourself," Ted Flint said, "next time."

Duncan turned. His limbs felt queerly heavy, and his head light, his ears singing. He had to make an effort to lift his feet up and put them down again, to get himself over the shingle. He carried the newspaper parcel just as Ted Flint had given it to him, flat across his outstretched hands. Next time, he had said, come and catch it for yourself next time. Next time, next time, next time . . .

When he reached the cottage and stood beside the unfinished wall in the drizzle, he remembered that he had not thanked Ted Flint for the fish.

* * *

In the hut, Davey Ward said, "You want looking at," drinking his tea, "you and all. You'll do no good there, I can tell you."

Ted Flint shrugged, grinning. "I'm not bothered."

"He's a case, that's what. Him and his mother. You're wasting your time."

Ted Flint kicked his boot against the bench. "Yes," he said. "That mother. Bloody old witch."

"What's it to you, then?"

"Nothing. No."

"Get him in your boat, he'd be lost, he'd be like an animal, you'd lose him over the side, that's what. He's not fit."

"He's all right."

"Never."

"He's *all right*, I said. There's no harm in him."

"No harm, no. I never said so, did I? Harm. But he's like a baby, he's frightened of his own shadow, you see that. There's nothing up here, nothing inside. He'd never manage."

"He manages."

"Does what Hilda Pike tells him."

"Yes."

"Well, and without her, then? Nothing. He'd do *nothing*, he'd be finished, they'd have to send him away, they'd put him in a home."

"No."

"They would."

"He'd do." Ted Flint stepped to the door and slung out the dregs of his tea mug, looked at the sky. "Getting up a bit now."

"I don't know what you bother for." Davey Ward stood up. "All of a sudden."

"It does no harm."

"You leave well alone, take my advice. You'll only make trouble. She wants nothing and nobody, that woman."

"Her! It's not her, is it?"

"We tried. All of us. We tried years ago. You wouldn't remember."

"I do."

"Leave well alone. You take him on, there'll be trouble." Davey Ward walked out of the hut. "Ask your own mother."

"It's nothing." Ted Flint turned away. "I'm not that bothered, you needn't take on."

Though he thought of the peaky, child's face of Duncan Pike, and felt sorry enough for him, would have done something. It didn't matter. He locked the door of the hut and picking up his bicycle swung a leg over. It was still raining.

* * *

In the cottage on Tide Street, Hilda Pike made him drop the fish, still wrapped up, into the dustbin.

"We eat our fish Wednesday," she said. "We buy what we want and we take nothing, not from anyone. You know."

He had smelled the beginning of the storm the previous day, as the others had. The wind had been driving blizzards inland, down the county, to the west. Now, that morning, turning to look back at the top of Church Hill, Duncan saw the sky. Over the sea, there was still a wash of light blue, the horizon glinted. But the sun had risen out of a red sky, and above the river, the clouds were massing together, liver-coloured, the marshes were dark as iron. Duncan felt uneasy. But the wind was still only roughening the surface of the sea.

By lunchtime, it had veered round abruptly and begun to blow a gale. Duncan could barely stand against it, he moved in closer to the shed. Cragg had set him on to sawing wood. Snow came in flurries for five or ten minutes at a time, hard and stinging against his face, and then was carried off again on the wind.

Cragg ate through his sandwiches and drank his tea, said nothing at all. They had tied the door to, with a piece of string. The Big House was empty, Mrs Reddingham-Lee had gone away.

Down the slopes in the houses of Heype, window-sashes began to loosen, the panes bumping softly, front gates rammed hard shut. Duncan went back to his logs. Half an hour later, the sky was dense as stone, and the red roof of the Big House was thick with gulls, making inland from the sea. At four, the town was almost dark. The sea was racing in fast, the waves coming down hard and harder on to the beach. The huts were almost empty. Nobody had been out all day. Davey Ward fiddled with a sprat net and hovered in his hut doorway, looking at the sky.

Coming into the shed where Duncan was putting the

saw away, ready for home, Cragg said, "Be rough tonight."

Duncan was suddenly afraid. Every winter he dreaded the storms, because of the noise they made, the tearing and crashing, but most of all he was afraid simply of his own fear at what they might do. He had watched the animals, seen cats flatten back their ears and slink away close to the walls, and the dogs lifting up their heads without warning, to howl. All over the marshes now, seabirds were coming in, they huddled together in the lee of old rowing-boats, and among the clumps of reed, and inland, wild hares raced for shelter among the gorse, fur flying.

He had always waited for their cottage to be washed away, he had imagined the great waves thundering down and tearing the bricks up like roots of a tooth, sucking the whole street up inside itself. For it had happened, people talked about it. Once, Tide Street had been quite far back, almost in the centre of the town, and through various terrible winters, and spring tides, the land had crumbled away, whole streets had dissolved like paper and the sea had sluiced over and flooded the river and the marshes for miles inland. In summer, he walked along the defence wall on clear, still nights, and thought of it, of the houses lying at the bottom of the sea, of chairs and tables and beds and ornaments which had been valuable to people, and of the cold steeples of churches. Though it was hard to remember what the storms were like then, when the air was warm under the risen moon.

Turning out of Market Street, he was almost lifted up and sent spinning, by the gale. The awning over Lunt's pie shop rattled, loose from one of its chains.

He dared not go and look at the sea, he could hear it booming on the shingle, the spray was blowing down Wash Alley into his face. His legs went weak suddenly, as he thought of the great press of waves beating up towards the house, and of how fragile everything was, rock and brick and the bones of people, fine as splinters against the force of it. He thought of the whole of England, as he had seen it on maps, spilled completely over by the sea, the edges eaten away like a biscuit, smaller and smaller and then swallowed, there would be no trace left. His mind sheered away from it, and he opened the door and was pushed hard by the wind behind him, into the front room.

On the beach, Davey Ward stood beside the lifeboat for a moment, lifted his hand up to touch the polished wood. Already the waves were high up beyond the stakes, roaring over the last shelf of pebbles, and the tide had two hours to go.

In the coastguard station, Joss Flack made a circle on a chart, looked at the direction of the arrows, and then out to sea again, rubbed his thumbs about over the pads of his fingers, waited. All afternoon, the trawlers had been moving fast along the horizon, making for port.

A wave lifted and toppled, and the foam seethed about the breakwater, the windows of the lookout were mizzled with spray.

In the cottage at the top of King Lane, Ted Flint stirred, straightening and recrossing his legs, listening to the gale, over the sounds of music on the television. Just before eight, he went out.

Black and White minstrels strutted and danced, and Alice Flint went on watching them and knitting, blank-eyed, thinking of nothing.

Inland, power cables came down, the lights went out in farmhouses and cottages out beyond Heype. As Ted Flint walked down the hill towards the Ship Inn, it began to sleet.

"You're to cut your toe-nails tonight," Hilda Pike said, "after you've had a bath."

Duncan's hand was still for a second, holding the reel of thin cotton he used to make the rigging. The radio played Viennese Waltzes from the Palm Court. She would not have a television set inside the cottage.

The ship was five and a half inches high and almost finished. It weighed nothing, balanced on his hand. He soaked the labels off matchboxes, saved for him by Cragg and Old Beattie and Mrs Reddingham-Lee, and then razored the wood finely, and used spent matches themselves, too, varnished and painted. The sails worked by a system of thread pulleys, each one could be individually raised and lowered. He was working from a picture of the Victory, torn from a magazine he had found beside the dustbins at the Big House.

"Did you hear?"

"Wine, Woman and Song" came waltzing out of the radio ball-room.

"It's time," she said, "it's past nine o'clock. You get the water boiling, leave that thing alone, now, I'm not having you slovenly in your habits. And you can do your hair, at the same time."

There was a rushing noise inside his head, it came up fast to the surface and boiled over, and he smashed his fist down like a chopper, crushing the tiny wood and cotton model, like a thin-winged fly, between itself and the table. Everything in the room shook slightly, and then resettled. Beyond the window, in Tide Street, the roar of the gale and the sea.

Hilda Pike did not speak.

Eventually, he lifted his hand up very gently and began to detach the broken pieces from where they had stuck to his palm. The edge of a splinter had sunk into the pulpy flesh at the base of his thumb. He took no notice of it. When he had gathered everything up together, he cupped his hand to the edge of the table and swept the bits and threads into it, and then walked two steps across the room, to drop them into the blazing centre of the fire. They vanished in a single lick of flame. Then the log burned on.

Hilda Pike's fingers flick-flicked ceaselessly in and out of the crochet.

"You think I've forgotten." She did not look up at him. "Or else you've forgotten. But I haven't. I don't forget. You think I don't know, but I knew how it would be from way back. I knew. I'd only to look at your face."

He had not moved, he was still looking down into the fire. "They sent you home from school. They put a note in your pocket and they sent you home with it. Weren't going to have that, were they? And can you blame them? And I had to go up there and talk them round, into taking you back. Yes, you may have forgotten, but I never shall. I knew. You can't change, you'll never change, not inside yourself. You don't *try*, Duncan Pike."

His head was clear, as though it had been rinsed through with ice-cold water, everything was sharper and brighter, her voice echoed like thin, high shouts, through a cave.

He had not forgotten.

There had been big glass jars of paint, and he was allowed to spoon some of it and set it around the edges of the old plate, one thick blob at a time, he might have any colours he liked, but no more than three. They painted, once a fortnight only, everything else was cleared off the low tables, and over their own clothes they wore special old shirts, made for the school by the mother of Miss Napp.

He could draw all day, filling page after page, using pencil after pencil, he would go on, never lifting his eyes up, not hearing if they told him to stop. But the paint alarmed him, it was something entirely different, looser and more slippery, something he could never quite control. He always bent down very close to the paper, and used the end of the brush, finely pointed like a pencil, to make little, elaborate marks, working in a single small corner. The others gouged out violent colours and spread them on like jam, bending the bristles of their paint-brushes and rubbing it all about.

But only three colours at a time. He had stood in silence, knowing what he wanted and overcome by the largeness of the glass pots and the bright white and blue, the emerald and nasturtium and scarlet, so that in the end Miss Napp had lost patience and told him which to choose, and helped him to them, blob, blob, blob, on the china plate, like runny ice-cream.

He had wanted to paint a haystack. Last week, they had all gone by bus out to a farm near Bloxhall, and he had seen one, it was the only thing he could, for certain, remember the shape of. He wanted to make a haystack, square and yellow and huge as a house, over all the sheet of paper, a haystack on green grass under a sky-blue sky.

He stared down at the china plate. Miss Napp had given him white and black and purple.

For a long time he stared, and did not know what he might do, he was entirely bewildered, unable to make new plans on the ruins of the old ones. And then he had lifted the plate and brought it down upon the table, smash, smash, smash, and knocked the pieces off, ground his feet again and again into them, so that the white and black and purple slurred together and came off on the crepey soles of his sandals in a dark mess, mixed up with chips of the china.

They had sent him home, with a note in his pocket, and he had never done anything like it again, never behaved violently except in secret, beating the rushes down or grinding two pebbles viciously together, somewhere by himself.

Now, the ship model was broken and burned.

"I don't know what's happening, Duncan Pike. Something's happening. I watch you. I know your face."

He bent down and took up another pear log and laid it carefully, at an angle, across the fire. The draught raced over the room from under the front door, sending the flames up at once, to cradle round it, catching the bark alight.

He said, "I'd best put the kettle on, then."

Hilda Pike did not reply. Then, there were the footsteps, and a rapping upon the door.

Ted Flint was like a giant in the front room, Duncan saw him beside the oak dresser and it seemed to him that he would be able to lift his hand and bring it down and crush them entirely, as he himself had just crushed the ship model.

His mother had gone still, the crochet resting on her lap, her eyes hard and bright as beads.

Ted Flint laughed. "I thought, why not take Duncan? Get the lad out for an hour." He looked across the room. "Are you coming then? I'll buy you a jar, our Duncan, down at the Ship."

Duncan's eyes widened. He did not move. Someone might have struck him a blow on the side of the head. Ted Flint's voice came and went like the sea, faded very far away. But his first instinct was to be afraid, to try and discover a reason. What had happened, all of a sudden? Come out in the boat. Come down to the Ship. *Why?* He was not to blame, yet it all seemed to have begun inside himself. *Why?* Though the rest of him would have done anything, gone anywhere, would trust Ted Flint entirely.

"Have an hour off," he said. "Why not? It's a rough night."

Music still came from the radio, a man's voice singing about a Merry Donkey.

"Come on, get your coat on, Duncan, why don't you?"

There was the same air of amusement about him, the same look, smoothed over his face like butter. Duncan thought, he doesn't care, he's not afraid of her, he can stand there and look down at her and she is nothing. And it seemed to him more than ever bewildering, that Ted Flint was as he was and had been away but come back, and now he stayed here in Heype, free as a bird.

"Hey?"

For a second, there was nothing, there was silence, even from the beating of the gale. Then, Hilda Pike had launched herself forward, the wheelchair was spinning across the room towards Ted Flint, and she had her stick up, waving it at him, beating it in the air, so that Duncan thought she would have rammed it into his face. Her voice was rising higher and higher as she spoke, raucous as a bird. Duncan shrank back against the wall in shame and terror. "You get away from here, Ted Flint, you get out, don't you bring yourself into this house again. Leave us alone, you leave us alone. Get out!"

Ted Flint stood his ground, though Duncan could see his body tensed under the oilskins, wondered what he might do.

"He doesn't go drinking, he doesn't go anywhere,

does he? Who do you think you're asking, Ted Flint? You know about him. He's nothing to do with any of you."

She was pressed up against him in her chair, and now she jabbed the stick forwards, it would have gone into his thighs. "You get out, don't you come banging on this door again, making trouble. You leave him be."

Ted Flint lifted a hand, took hold of the stick and twisted it lightly out of her grasp, then threw it, at floor level, across the room. It skidded to rest underneath the window.

"It's what you need, boy," he said quietly, "I tell you. Get your coat on, I'll buy you a jar."

He spoke in the same, slow, laughing voice. He did not care, Hilda Pike might not have been there, he thought nothing of her. She turned the wheelchair round in a half-circle, to face Duncan. The bass voice sang out roundly from the wireless.

"You go out of here with him, Duncan Pike, and you don't come back." He knew that she meant it. None of them spoke again.

When Ted Flint opened the door, Duncan thought the sea had come up into the garden, everything was roaring. He shrank away, back towards the kitchen door.

After a long time, he looked up at her. She had not moved in the chair. Now, she reached out a hand and pointed to where her stick lay under the window on the floor. Her face was grey-white, her eyes oddly distended, and as though they had sunk further back in her head. Duncan went across the room slowly, and got the stick.

"You can take me to bed now. You can do it before your bath. I'm ready to go to bed. My back hurts."

He handed the stick to her and took the rug off her knees, and folded it, and then lifted his mother very gently, carried her upstairs.

"You're mad!"

"You can tell him." Davey Ward tapped the stem of his pipe against his front teeth. "I have, I've told him, over and again. He's wasting his time and he'll lay up trouble. Why bother? What's it all in aid of, I want to know? All of a sudden. *I've* told him. You may as well save your breath."

Ted Flint raised the mug of beer and drank from it easily, grinned.

"What's it all about?"

"Nothing," he said. "Nothing special."

"You ask Old Beattie Thorpe. She knows, she'll tell you. Knew her as a girl, knew the family. She'd tell you."

"It's not like you, either, Ted Flint."

"No."

"No — well, mind yourself, then."

Ted shook his head, still laughing. The bar was full of men now, the air thick with pipe smoke.

"You'd lose him in here, that young Duncan, he'd slip down a crack in the table, like half of him slipped down his mother's leg, day he was born. He'd not know what to do with himself."

"He'd learn."

Davey Ward hissed. Beyond the windows, across the square, the sea.

"A foreigner, he was," Bert Malt said.

"What?"

"That Duncan Pike's father."

"So they say." Ted Flint had never believed it.

"Oh yes. Came off one of the trawlers at Lowestoft. Ask Old Beattie."

"With Hilda Pike? Never!"

"She'd legs to use in those days, hadn't she?"

"Get on."

"There's plenty up there that knew her. He's only your age, Ted Flint, it's not so long ago."

"Long enough."

"Well, he was a foreigner. They're not fussy."

"He'd not need to be."

Ted Flint lifted a fresh glass of beer. "She is," he said. "She'd be fussy."

Davey Ward stood up. The others waited.

"I'll go out and take a look at it."

They parted for him, standing back from the draught as the door opened.

Ted Flint went over to the darts board, forgetting about Duncan Pike, waiting, like the rest, for high water, for what the storm might do. But, coming here, along Tide Street, he had remembered her face as she came at him across the tiny room. He thought, she'd kill you. Or him. She'd take that stick to anyone. She would.

Davey Ward came back inside, hair and face streaming with water. He took the pipe, still lighted, out of his pocket again, said nothing. Ted Flint sent the dart off and into the board, for a double.

He waited until she had gone to sleep. But she was tired, she had slipped down between the heavy blankets like some frail insect, it was hardly any time.

As he pulled on the raincoat and boots and woollen gloves, he was trembling, his heart thudded when he bent down. He wore nothing on his head, and when he got outside he hunched himself up, leaning forwards into the gale. All the way there, he stayed close to the wall.

The Ship stood back from the square, behind the lifeboat memorial, open to the sea. It was crashing up high over the defence wall, now, the noise was like thunder, the air heavy with sleet and blown spume.

He skirted round the back of the pub, his rubber boots silent and slippery on the cobbles, and then on the belt of muddy grass. When he came up to the bar window, he pressed himself as hard as he could against the wall, edging up step by small step, nearer to the light.

At first, he could see nothing for the flying mist in the air, and hear nothing above the gale. He waited, shivering. He thought, I could have gone with him, he asked me, he came for me, I could have gone. Though he scarcely believed it.

Then the sounds began to detach themselves, a wave of laughter and a single voice calling across the bar, somebody banging. The low room was brown-yellow, and all the men were blue, their shadows falling darkly together across tables and walls and floor. He saw Ted Flint's back, the fair hair curling low over his collar.

He could not have gone in, not even in Ted Flint's company, the sight of all the men there together terrified him, he smelled the strange smell of the place even from the outside, like an animal scenting danger. He would not have been able to stand there or speak or move. But he had had the chance.

He took his hand out of his pocket and held it against the brick, pressing it, trying to feel the warmth from within. He thought, I could do anything.

In the cottage on Tide Street, Hilda Pike slept.

Later, when he did come home, cold and stiff from holding his body so hard to the wall, he boiled the kettles and bathed himself in the tin bath, as she had told him.

They had been expecting it, all of them. Davey Ward had gone uneasily to sleep, downstairs on the sofa, keeping his clothes on, and there were others, too, all about the town. In the coastguard station, Joss Flack moved his hand every so often towards the telephone, silent in its black cradle, heard bells that did not ring, and saw imaginary flames hurtle up into the tossing sky.

The tide lashed up and over the defence wall, spilling across the street and slavering like tongues down between the alleys, and then it turned back, furiously into itself. It began to snow, the flakes caught up and whirled about crazily by the gale.

Duncan woke seconds before he heard the boom of the first, and then, at once, the second, maroon, and he could not lie there, he got out of bed and began to dress and did not bother to see if the noise had wakened his mother, before he ran from the cottage.

Some of the men were already there and the others came racing down the slopes, pulling on oilskins, it was almost a relief, they had been waiting so long for something to happen. It had come. The arc-lamps were switched on, so that the lifeboat and a stretch of the beach glowed like an island, the air full of flying water, fading away into the blackness at the edges.

By the time Duncan got there, they were all up in the lifeboat, men were moving swiftly about below, and inside the shed, he saw Davey Ward lean over the side, shouting something hoarsely. He was mesmerized by the speed of it all, and by the way they knew what to do, did not have to stop and think and put one foot carefully in front of the other.

It seemed that everyone in Heype had come out, they stood huddled in overcoats and oilskins, behind the lifeboat. Duncan rushed forward to see, careless of who they were. He jumped off the wall on to the shingle and was knocked sideways by the force of the wind, into one of the wooden huts. As he looked up again, the lifeboat shot forward down the slipway and hit the sea, sending great sheets of water up on either side, which extended, creaming over and over along the top. The boat dropped down steeply and then climbed again, dropped and climbed, disappearing almost at once into the darkness.

It was bitterly cold. There were people along the wall, and across the street near the Ship, and in the shelter of the memorial. Duncan stood by himself beside the hut, he wanted to wait and see the boat in again. For some reason he was not, now, so afraid of the noise and the storming sea. He could not have gone back into the cottage and lain in bed, in the room next to his mother.

But after a time, he did move, wanting to be nearer to people, began to edge along the wall. As he stepped down from it, opposite the Ship, he saw Ted Flint's mother.

Once, years before, she had come to the cottage on Tide Street, with a freshly baked pie, had offered to push out the wheelchair, to do some washing. Hilda Pike had sent him to the door and made him say no, no, we don't take anything from anyone, we don't need charity, you leave us, all of you, leave us be. She had sat behind him in the shadows of the room, listening, as he stammered out what he could of the phrases she had taught him. Alice Flint had left the pie on the doorstep, wrapped in a white cloth.

"You take that back. You get your coat on and go up there, tell her. You do it now."

He had wandered miserably about the alleys of Heype, with his hands full of the wrapped pie, unable to do as she had told him and return it, and desperate because he did not know what else he might do. In the end, he had walked miles inland, until he was sure of not being seen from the town and then had dropped it into the river, plate and cloth, everything, and watched it sink like a stone. But the white cloth had detached itself after a moment, and got caught up among the reeds, and he had taken to his heels, run away from it in alarm, certain that it would be discovered, and that Ted Flint's mother would come to punish him. And his own mother had been waiting in the doorway.

"You — where do you think you've been all this time, what have you been doing? That's an hour, over an hour. You tell me what you've done."

But he had not.

"Did you take that pie back to her? Did you?"

He had turned his back on her, nodded.

"And tell her what I said?"

"I . . . it's gone now. Gone."

He did not know if she believed him.

Now, he saw Mrs Flint watching him. She had come running down from King Lane after her son, with his sea boots and another jersey, one of the men had thrown them up to him in the lifeboat.

Duncan's head filled up with all the things he should say to her, and with everything he remembered, the stories people had told him about the death of Ted Flint's father and grandfather, in the old lifeboat, the thought of the meat pie dissolving in the river, the way his own mother had spoken. For a moment, he opened his mouth and his tongue locked, he could manage nothing, other people had come near to them, someone was talking about the trawler to which the lifeboat had gone. Snow and spray were driving, mingled together, across the open street.

"Mrs Flint . . ." Duncan said, and the words that came out of his mouth were strangely distorted, it was the old way he had used to talk, as a young child. "Mrs Flint . . ." She might not be able to understand him. He could have wept.

Alice Flint turned her head, as though she had only just become aware of him. She had a curiously loose, pulpy face, the features in it tiny, porcine, though she was not fat. There was a dead, shadowy look about her eyes, and then Duncan saw the anger rise up into them, her face was suffused with loathing of him.

"You? What do you want? What do you think you're doing, what use are you here, Duncan Pike? You're not fit to be out. Don't you come slinking round me."

He realized that she had not spoken to him once, since that day she had come to their door, he had forgotten what her voice sounded like. Now, he backed away from her, terrified, and overcome with guilt and shame, because she hated him, he had not gone out with the lifeboat, he was fit for nothing.

Ted Flint's father had died in front of her, a wave had hit the lifeboat as it came back in, so that it had turned over completely and would not right itself and the suction had pinned the men, helpless, inside. Duncan had heard the story, among all the others of death and drowning, as he grew up in Heype.

Nobody stopped him, going across the street, but when he reached the corner, opposite the Ship, he half-heard a voice calling his name, twice, three times. He did not stop or turn, he did not go back to the cottage, he ran.

As he went inland along the river bank, the roar of the sea gradually faded, but then the wind took over, sweeping across the open marshes, whistling through his head, so that he put up his hands and pressed them inwards to stop the pain in his ear-drums. He could see nothing ahead of him, but he scarcely needed to, he knew where he was going. Twice his feet slipped and he almost went down the bank into the water, the path was treacherous with ice and rain-soaked mud. It was not far. It seemed to take him hours. He lost sense of everything except the cold and wind and the remembrance of Mrs Flint's face, pushed into his, deriding him, the sound of what she had said.

Where the river bent round, there was a boat, in the groin of the bank. It had a wooden plank leading across to it. In the summer, he came and sat here, the boat belonged to no one, and it was sheltered, like the martello tower. Nobody could see him, no one else came.

Now, he went down on his hands and knees and crawled along the soaking wood. The boat rocked suddenly with his weight and movement, and the blast of the wind. He stopped, unable to see ahead or behind him. The river was high, rushing over the stones and choking the reeds below. Aloud, he said, "All right, all right," and the words were torn away as they came out of his mouth, like shreds of rag, into the whistling darkness, before they had a chance to reach his own ears, he only had the sensation of his mouth having moved, the idea of what he had said, to comfort him.

"All right . . . Duncan . . . Duncan . . ."

His hands came abruptly against the edge of the boat and he lifted one and then the next, up and over, and then his legs and body, climbed in. At once, he went up to his knees in water, the bottom of the old boat was full. But the wooden seats were only slimed with mud and snow. He hunched himself up on one of them, legs and arms tight together, and pressed his head down between his knees, shivering with relief. In spite of what it was like, of the total blackness and emptiness of the marshes and of the cold, he felt all right, felt safe. He was away from the crashing sea, and from the stares on the faces of the people, away from Mrs Flint.

The wood of the boat smelled sweet and damp and rotten. There were no oars, it had been here for years, bumping against the bank, disintegrating. In spring and early summer, it was full of nesting birds. He had seen a heron poised on the prow of it, still as stone, waiting for fish. Then, the wood dried out in the sun, it was bleached grey.

All right, he said again, all right, and slipped down further, thinking of nothing. He did not sleep but there were several hours during which he sat in a half-trance, his mind and body were numb, he was uncertain where he was or what had happened to him.

On the beach, people waited, sat about uselessly by the walls of houses. Alice Flint walked home, spoke to no one. In kitchens and bedrooms up the town, lights stayed on. Old Beattie sat in one of the green municipal shelters, beside the memorial, bellied out in places like a sail, with the newspaper tied about her underneath the raincoat, remembering the faces of Ted Flint's mother, and Duncan Pike, running away.

Eight miles out, the Heype lifeboat reached the sinking trawler and began the job of taking men off, in the gale. They must come in close enough but without grinding the two boats together. Ted Flint wiped an arm across his face as they swung back, waited for the sea, tried again.

In the cottage on Tide Street, Hilda Pike slept.

* * *

He came to very slowly. It was still dark, but the gale had died down a little. The snow was falling steadily now, his hair and the shoulders and arms of his coat were covered with it. He unclenched the fingers of each hand, one by one, moved himself inside the coat like a tortoise waking within a shell. At first he was bewildered. There had been the log fire and his broken ship model burning in it, and his mother's stick, spinning away across the floor, he knew that he had carried her upstairs and put her to bed . . .

Then, recollection came pouring down through his head like a waterfall, people's faces and voices, the way the sea had parted and lifted up on either side of the lifeboat.

He began to scramble up and out of the old boat, in a panic. But he was stiff and cold, so that he slipped about, fell twice, soaking himself and pushing a splinter into his hand, from the wooden plank. When he tried to run along the river path, he fell again on the snow that lay on top of the mud and grass and his face went into a clump of it. He was not hurt, only shaken and covered with a cold mess of yellow soil and snow.

He did not know the time but it was dark until late, these mornings. Perhaps he should have the breakfast ready, now, and his own flask and sandwiches, his mother should be out of bed and dressed, perhaps he should already be at the Big House. Or it might still be the middle of the night.

He made his way unsteadily to the end of the path and crossed the last stretch of marshy grass, to climb up on to the sea wall. Half of his mind was still blocked off, he wondered if he were really outside and why he should be stumbling about in the snow. The nerves pricked and tingled under the skin of his face. He wanted to go to bed and sleep. But when he looked up again, he saw that it was getting light, the sky above the sea was the colour of pewter, he could make out the shape of the first buildings at the end of Tide Street. He thought, they must have come back, it's all finished, it's the morning now. *They must have come back.* And he went away from the cottage and down the nearest alley, out on to the beach.

The storm was blowing itself out, but the sea was still rough and laced with white, the tide starting to come in again. The pebbles ground together beneath his feet, under a soft layer of snow, and as the light spread up over Heype, it gleamed white in the roof groins. Duncan tried to make his legs move more quickly, along the beach, but they were aching from the hours he had spent huddled up in the old boat. The bones of his head ached too, as though the snow had been absorbed right into them, like water into a sponge.

He heard a shout, and then a reply to the shout, and looked up. He was a hundred yards away from the point where they launched the lifeboat. He stopped dead. The first light was eerie, and the sky hung heavy with snow, though very little was falling.

The lifeboat had come in, and was grounded at the water's edge, they had laid down the flat wooden skids over which to haul it back up the steep shingle, now that the tide was low. Near it, a few men stood close together. But the rest of the people were still up on the wall, and in the street behind the fishermen's huts, watching. It seemed to Duncan that none of them had moved at all since he had run away from them, and from the voice of Mrs Flint. Now, he did not go any nearer. She was still there, her coat the colour of a holly berry, in the blue-greyness.

He thought, I have to go home, go home, and he began to shake his head, to try and clear out the frozen feeling, understand what he must do. The knot of men stirred, then moved apart, and then closed together again. Bert Malt came walking down the beach and joined them. A man in oilskins began to climb slowly down from the boat, then stopped half-way, clinging to the ladder like a yellow butterfly on a wall. After a time, he climbed back again.

Duncan did not move.

It was a long while before they were ready to lift the two bodies down, on stretchers, and covered over with sheets, and carry them slowly up the beach. The sky was paler, like flaked fish.

"What was all that about? Running away?"

He started. She always did this, Old Beattie, appeared suddenly beside him, as though she needed to be mysterious.

"What's Alice Flint done to you?"

He stammered, the words meaningless.

Beattie shook her head. "She meant nothing. It's only what she says. She won't remember that this morning."

He looked over towards the open square, and saw the holly berry coat somewhere, and then it was blocked in by all the others again, by grey and navy-blue, moving off towards the town.

"They lost three," Beattie Thorpe said. "That was him they brought, Ted Flint. And one from off the trawler. But they lost another, over the side."

The snow began to swirl thickly again, through the air, he could not see far ahead across the shingle.

"Get home, Duncan Pike, look at you, you're half frozen. Get on home."

But he waited without moving, until they had brought the lifeboat itself up, hauling it on the capstan inch by inch over the skids, through driving snow. He thought of the things he could have done, if he had been one of the men, knowing his place, and what to say and do.

After a time, everyone went away. He watched Old Beattie, pushing through the snowstorm. He had never seen her without the pram before.

When he reached the cottage his mother was still asleep, there had been no sound through the house to disturb her. Always, he woke first, and took her cup of tea, the noise of his footsteps or the opening of the door were what woke her.

He did everything just as usual, and then left for work, and he did not speak to her once, not even in answer to the stream of angry remarks and questions, the talk about last night, and the way he had gone mad with himself and burned the model ship, the arrival of Ted Flint. He wondered if she would lift her stick to him, in the end, to try and beat him into speaking to her. She said, "I know you, I know what you're like. Nobody else knows you, you don't know yourself, but I do."

He did not answer, though he could think very clearly now, the numbness had all gone, and one part of his mind fed orders to him, said, fill the kettle, strike the match, watch the toast, lift, open, close, come, go, so that it was easy, he obeyed, just as he obeyed Cragg. Ted Flint was dead, they had brought his body up from the lifeboat on a stretcher, covered in a white sheet, and there was nothing more to think about it.

"Get down that cellar," Cragg said, "get your boots on, it's flooded with water in one corner. And the shed roof's half off, as well."

He did not ask about Duncan's lateness. Duncan did as he was told, worked the whole day on the storm damage to the house, his head empty of all thought. He did not speak to Cragg, either.

That day they had to eat their lunch in the garage, and once, Cragg lifted his eyes from the newspaper, to give Duncan a queer look. After a moment, he said, "I saw you. Down on the beach. I saw you." But there was no expression in his voice.

Duncan went on eating through his cheese sandwich.

It snowed all that afternoon, while Cragg was up on the roof of the toolshed, hammering the broken wood back into place. Duncan stood about below, handing up tools. They had cleared the water out of the cellar, there was, Cragg said, nothing else for him to do. His fingers were swollen and blue with cold, poking out of the ends of the half mittens.

Inside the Big House, everything was silent, the covers straight and smooth upon beds, cushions plump and undisturbed. Major and Mrs Reddingham-Lee had gone abroad, on a ship from Southampton.

Last summer, Cragg had been off for two days, sick. In the top greenhouse, Duncan had hosed down tomatoes, smelling the dry, sweet smell of the fruit and the dark-green leaves, hot under the glass. The fine spray went pattering softly down through them, glinting as it dried on the shiny skins. He had felt happy, though anxious at being alone, not to have Cragg giving him orders. And then, Mrs Reddingham-Lee had gone out, he had watched her leave the house by the side door, and climb into her eggshell-blue car. She had worn a hat and driven up the hill, away from the town.

Duncan had laid down the hosepipe and gone out of the conservatory. The sun beat down on to the pale paving of the steps, and reflected up again into his face, burning it. Behind him, in a thin line down between the houses, the sea, polished bright as enamel.

There was nobody else in the house. When he closed the door of the kitchen and stood in the wide hall, everything seemed to settle around him, it was entirely still. The sun came through a round pane of glass in the front door. He began to go about the place, very quietly, into every room, feeling the different feel under his shoes, smelling the strange smells. There was pale waxed wood and the thick knotted pile of rugs, the colours of the drawing-room were gold and white and lemon in the sun. He had touched things gently, feeling the texture of silk cushions, roughened against his skin, lifting up a paper knife from the desk beside the window and balancing it. Upstairs, the bedroom overlooked the empty garden.

It had wide windows and corn-coloured curtains, and smelled of Mrs Reddingham-Lee, as though her scented powder hung about on the air. He was inquisitive about everything here, wanting to touch each chair and picture and ornament, to open cupboards and drawers and stare inside. But he had moved about cautiously, his nerves alert just below the skin, hearing the seething of the dust. He thought, this is what they have, this and this and this, here is where they eat, and laugh and sit and sleep, this is all of theirs. He had never seen what it was like before. The rooms were all long and high and bright with the afternoon sun, but he felt as though, if he breathed out too quickly, the things about him might splinter and break. He touched his fingers slowly down on to the white piano keys and they were cool, the notes sounded faintly, vibrating far away down the strings. He wanted to stay here. Outside, he saw the shimmer of heat over the garden.

After a long time, he had gone and the rooms had settled back into themselves again, when he looked behind him anxiously, he could see no trace of his own presence there.

When he was fumbling to tie back some raspberry canes, Mrs Reddingham-Lee returned. Watching her put her legs out of the blue car, and stand up, he thought, I know everything about you, I know secrets. Though later he had realized that it was nothing, that he knew only curtains and tables and vases and chairs, the smell of a bedroom. Nothing.

Now, the wind came whipping suddenly up the lawn, blowing the snow about in tiny, stinging particles. Cragg began to make his way cautiously down from the roof of the shed, his legs first, waving over the edge. Duncan put up an arm to steady him. Cragg grunted.

Higher up the coast, the body of the other man from the trawler was washed ashore.

"You can get off home early," Cragg said. "There's no more to do in this, and you're fit for nothing. Up half the night. I saw you."

But Duncan took a long time putting the tools away, collecting up his flask and empty sandwich box, so that it was almost dark by the time he reached the bottom of the hill and turned left into King Lane, he could see the light on in the front room of the Flints' cottage. For the first time since the previous night, he began to be afraid, thinking of what he was going to do.

Esther Ward was there. She had been at the house very early in the morning, to lay the body out, and now she had come back, to make cups of tea for callers and poke the fire, and to look time after time at Alice Flint, waiting for nothing.

She twitched the curtain. He stood close up to the door after knocking, shoulders hunched, his hair stuck about with melting flakes of snow.

She said, "Duncan Pike."

Alice Flint looked up, eyes small and dull in the puffy face. On the dresser behind her stood the photographs, and the small oak plaques, the bronze medals awarded posthumously. The fire was banked, black with fresh coal, smoking hard.

"Have I to let him in?"

She shrugged.

The last of the daylight slipped down suddenly, beyond the window.

"He ought to be put away," Alice Flint said. "You saw him, last night, mooning about. The two of them ought. What sort of a life is that? What sort of a man is he going to be? Cooking and pushing her about and treated like a baby. He *is* a baby, always was. They went to the same school, didn't they, they were in the same class. He told me. Duncan Pike was ten years old before he could write his own name. Ten years old. And I wouldn't trust him, that one, he'd be violent, he'd do anything that came into his head. Wouldn't he? You can't tell me. You've only to look at his face. What use is he to anyone?"

Esther Ward stood by the door, hearing her out, making no comment. He had not knocked again, nor had he gone away, he was still hunched up there waiting, like a dog.

A green-blue flame licked up through the coal, and died again. "Oh, let him in." Alice Flint turned her head away. "Do what you like. It's nothing to me."

Esther Ward went to open the door.

Coming here, down the street, he had wondered what he would say, how he might ask, though he knew it was all right, it was what other people did. He remembered when John Dent had come to school and told them about his dead grandfather, laid out and on display in their front parlour, in the open coffin. "You could come," he had said to Duncan, "everybody comes. They take their hats off and pray a prayer over him, that's all. Anybody can come and look. It's his dead body. But if you want to come, you'll have to give me threepence first."

Duncan had not gone, because he was afraid, remembering the terrible stories they told him, and because he had not liked John Dent's grandfather, with the huge dark warts upon his neck. Besides, his mother never let him have money.

Standing in the snow, he wondered what he should say, how to ask, and began to tremble, the muscles in his stomach and down his legs tightened, and tightened, like pulled wires. Alice Flint. She might do anything, might spit in his face, or hit him, might shout and curse and send him away. But although it was a long time before the door opened, he did not think to leave.

He was startled by Davey Ward's wife.

"It's . . . . Ted Flint," he said, in the end, stammering, "I came to see him. I came to see."

"Yes."

She paused, looking at him narrowly, and then turned, saying nothing more, and began to go ahead of him up the dark stairs. The door of the bedroom was closed. When she opened it, she did not go in, but stood to one side, letting him pass.

He had not known what he would do, had felt nothing all the way here. The light from the lamp beside the bed, and from overhead, was very bright. Through a slit in the curtains he could see the snow, gleaming like bone on the flat roof of the outhouse. Esther Ward remained in the doorway, watching him.

When the lifeboat had turned and come in for the third time, a wave had caught them sideways on, tipping the boat and crashing down over the deck. Coxswain Davey Ward, clinging to the wheel and blinded by the streaming water, had seen nothing. Then, the side of the lifeboat had ground up hard against the trawler. When he had wiped his eyes, he saw that Ted Flint had been washed off his feet and half-way over the rail, to have his body caught before it could fall down into the sea, and pinned against the other boat. They had reached and held him, pulled him back on to the lifeboat deck. He had died on the way back to Heype, among the rescued men from the trawler.

Duncan opened his eyes, when he felt his knees come up against the side of the bed. He looked down. He had not expected to see anything except a cold, white thing, sheeted, dead as a fish. But he saw Ted Flint, his hair and the rough surface of his skin were the same, except for the plaster and bandage, and the dark abrasion just below his eye. He thought, this is all him, he is here, and he imagined the brain and heart and lungs packed tightly together within the bone cage, the red blood thick and still. He had imagined something transparent, ghostly as the snow, something that was called a corpse, but there was only the man, Ted Flint, huge and heavy, he could have put out his hand and touched and the skin and hair would have felt the same as his own felt.

He was shocked most of all by this. He did not move or speak, only cried without knowing it, the tears squeezing abruptly out under tight lids, and drying at once on his face. His hands were clenched tightly, until the bones ached, pressing into one another. He was silent.

By the door, Esther Ward waited, uneasy, not leaving

him because she had never trusted him, would be surprised at nothing he might do. But in the end, she said, "You'd best go home."

He started violently at the sound of her voice in the tiny bedroom. On the dressing table, and the top of the chest, he could see things, Ted Flint's things, and he dared not look.

"Go on. Go home."

He went without a word, down the stairs and out of the door and along King Lane through the frozen snow, his head rinsed clean and clear, no longer afraid. Though by the time he reached Tide Street, anger had begun to pile up slowly within him, a dead weight.

"He cried," Esther Ward said, "that Duncan Pike. He's like a baby. Stood and cried."

Alice Flint turned around, her voice raised and wild, for the first time that day.

"Him? What's it to him? What does he know about it? He never knew anything. What did he have to cry about?"

And she put up her hands to her face and pressed them there, her eyes dry and burning, knowing suddenly what had happened, and that there was nothing left for her, no hope or future. She thought, I would kill him, he was in this house alive and I would have killed him, him or anyone.

The voice of a man came into the room, reading the news of the day from the flickering television. Alice Flint sat down dully and watched it.

The snow fell all that night and then froze, hard and

glittering between the cobbles down all the slopes of Heype, and lying bright and thin as glass, over the surface of the river.

The roof of the toolshed was mended. Cragg set Duncan on to sawing logs, more and more logs, they were piled up along the inner wall of the garage and labelled ash and holly, birch and pear. He worked steadily all through the days before the funeral, and at night, sat in the front room of the cottage in Tide Street and said nothing, did nothing, his head full with the picture of Ted Flint's body. Cragg watched him. In the mornings, Old Beattie stood on the beach with her pram and saw him walking up Church Hill. In the wheelchair, Hilda Pike worked at her white crochet furiously, so that the squares and circles were piled up on the table beside her, enough for a bedspread, enough to pack up in a parcel and send away. She made Duncan go, with one of the notes, written in black carpenter's pencil, down to the shop to buy more wool, and for the first time in his life, he found that he was unable to ask for what he wanted, he had forgotten, so that in the end he had fumbled about in his pocket and brought out the note, his face working in shame and anger. The woman, Dora Stevens, peered at him across the counter and bit back her question. alarmed, read the note and wrapped the crochet wool quickly, wanting him away.

He was not going to work, on the morning of the funeral, no one in Heype would work, people drew their curtains against the dazzling sun and went up to the church, waited.

He had a suit, folded in newspaper and laid across the

bottom of her wardrobe, a suit that had belonged to her father. It was navy-blue, pressed and flat, the jacket too wide for him, so that his shoulders sloped down and he looked oddly shrunken inside it.

"That's all right," Hilda Pike had said, "that's good stuff, best quality, you've no need for anything new for yourself, the few times you'll have occasion to wear it."

Which had been, the day he was interviewed at the Big House, by Mrs Reddingham-Lee, and then once a year, when they walked up to the church, on the anniversary of his grandmother's death.

Now, he saw himself, small and strange, looking in the wardrobe mirror, the bones of his wrists and fingers, cheeks and jaw, prominent just below the tight, pale flesh, eyes wide and blank-blue. He had made the breakfast and given it to his mother, put her in the wheelchair, beside the window, and had not spoken, not even to explain why he did not then go out to work. But he could not leave the house without being seen by her, he must come downstairs and cross the room, to reach the front door.

She had wheeled herself around, so that she was there in front of him, blocking the way. Her hair was scraped back more tightly than usual into the metal comb, so that the skin was taut, her eyes pulled upwards slightly at the corners.

"You can get my coat," she said, "the dark one, and help me on with it. You're to take me with you."

Duncan did not move.

"How often do I get the chance to see anything, go

anywhere? What company are you, going about the place like a daft thing, never saying a word? You don't know and you don't think and you don't care, you do what you like. I'm sorry I ever bore you."

"It's a funeral," he said slowly, "that's all. It's nothing you'd want to go to."

"How do you know what I want or don't want? How? You never ask. You know nothing."

"It's a funeral . . ."

"I know what it is, you don't have to tell me anything. I read things, don't I? I know better than you what goes on."

And that was no more than true, for she read the local paper like a vulture, was endlessly curious about the people of Heype with whom she wanted nothing to do. He was the one who went out into the town and talked to them and saw things, and he was the one who did not know.

"I want my coat, don't I? Coat and gloves and hat. You heard me."

He could do nothing. He did not want her to go, to be seen with her by everyone, the fishermen and Cragg and Alice Flint, to have to watch the coffins and listen to the words of the parson, in her presence.

But she was waiting, her lips parted slightly, leaning forward. He was still afraid of her. The front room felt cold. Duncan went back up the stairs and fetched the clothes, as she had told him, a pain drilling through his head.

It was hard and slow, pushing the wheelchair up the slopes, it stuck in the pavement ruts and on piles of frozen snow, skidded over the ice. The sky was washed a clear, bright blue and the sun shone. Hilda Pike sat under the rug in her chair, holding herself stiff against every jolt, her gloved hands on her lap. When they came up behind other people, she stared through them, said nothing. We keep ourselves to ourselves in this town.

The path was lined with schoolchildren in dark coats, waiting. The sunlight came into the broad nave of the church through plain glass windows, fell palely on the stone of the walls, and floor, and on the yellow brasses, everything was bare and bright and open, and Duncan was filled with alarm, wanting there to be dark places. He could be seen by everyone, all their eyes followed him, as he moved down the side aisle, pushing his mother.

When the coffins came, on the shoulders of other men from the boat, the lids were thick with yellow flowers, and as he saw them, he began to be afraid, waited for some terrible noise and for the lids to burst open, pouring blood, for thunder and lightning, and the roof of the church to creak and cave in on the heads of all the people. He wanted to hide his face, to crawl away, lie down on the stone floor beneath the dark wooden pews, so that he would be safe. The noise of the organ rushed loud as water through his head, and he shook it again and again, fearing that it would crack open like the fragile coffins. The sun was dazzling, on the altar rail. He saw his mother's hands, white and thin as his own, resting on top of the dark rug.

"All flesh is not the same flesh. But there is one kind of flesh for men, another flesh of beasts, another of fishes and another of birds . . ."

In his bursting head, he saw the bruise rotting on Ted Flint's face, the flesh, with its blue tattoos, peeling away from the bones, and then the dead white cod Davey Ward had sold him, lying heavy across his hands. He waited as the men lifted up the coffins again and began to move away, for the end of all the world, for his own flesh to split softly open, ripe as fruit.

When they had gone out, and around the path to the graves, he did not move. He had sat all the time, at the end of the pew, his bones locked together and the pain and confusion in his head. When the rest of them had stood and sang, knelt and prayed, he had not moved. Now, he wondered what had happened and why he was here, with the noises outside, muffled by the thick stone walls, and within, the breath left behind on the air, cooling, the dust motes sifting about in a band of sunlight, where the coffins had been.

She was watching him.

"Look at you! You're not safe to be out. What's the matter with you, Duncan Pike?"

He did not stir.

"You can take me back the long way. I've had enough. I've had enough of being in this place." She waited. "Get up, then. What's the matter with you?"

Outside, the sound of singing again, the voices of the schoolchildren, and the footsteps back up the path, then the empty cars, moving off. He thought again of the bodies, of how they were like his own body, thought how Ted Flint's skin and hair had looked, and the flesh, dense and opaque, the same as when he had stood in the front room in Tide Street, caring for nothing.

"You!"

He stood up and walked away, out of the church, opened, then closed the wooden door behind him. When she shouted, he took no notice. He heard the wheels of the chair skid round on the floor, but he had left before she could reach him, and then she was stuck, unable to lift herself over the single step.

Outside, ahead of him, he saw the backs of the children, two by two in file together, returning to school, and when he reached the corner of the church, there were the others, everyone bunched together, going down the hill, talking of the funeral. He crossed the road, and skirted the backs of the houses along Cliff Walk, then cut through an alley and down the steep steps that led from the top of the town right down into Market Street. The walls of the cliff rose up on each side, stone-faced, and green with moss. When he was small, he had been afraid to come here. There was no light until the bottom, no sunshine, even on the afternoons of midsummer. Now, the steps were deserted and icy, he held on to the iron rail and ran faster and faster as he neared the bottom. There was no more fear in him, no feeling for anything at all. He thought, I can do what I like, there is only me and I can do anything. Power surged through him like happiness. I can do what I like . . .

In the cottage he changed carefully out of the suit and replaced it between the sheets of newspaper, smoothing it all out. He put on his working jeans and shirt and jumper, and the navy-blue woollen jacket, he cut his sandwiches and filled the flask with tea, packed them into the holdall.

"There's that paint come today," Cragg said, "for the garden benches. You can go into the garage and make a start on them."

In the church, Hilda Pike was found, and pushed home by Old Beattie. Twenty years ago, they had worked side by side, in the sheds at Lowestoft, packing, had lived at either end of the same street, each had watched the other and discovered secrets, and they had never spoken. Now, Beattie Thorpe pushed the wheelchair and was not thanked for it, remembered Duncan's face in the church, knowing how he was, knowing everything about Hilda Pike. Saying nothing.

The sun shone all that day and in King Lane, Alice Flint sorted clothing in the empty back bedroom, to burn or sell or give away.

Duncan stayed on until after eight o'clock, in the Big House garage, the smell of new paint burning through his nostrils and down into his stomach as he bent his head close to the slatted garden benches. He felt curiously happy, knowing all the things he might do. Outside, the air shone with frost, and a blade-thin moon above the lime-tree.

He did not know what had happened to his mother, and now did not care. Though he knew that he should have gone home. Coming down the hill, he looked closely at all the houses, at the colour of the paint on their doors, the shape of the windows, and it was as if he had never seen them before. There was no one about in the streets. He crossed the square and stood on the defence wall, looking at the sea. It was very still, the surface glistening under the moon. He stepped down on to the shingle. The pebbles shone silver and white, and the dark heaps of fish nets, the roofs of the wooden huts were covered in rime, like snails' trail. The tide was coming in. Duncan felt again the rich, childish pride in himself, a wild excitement at what he might do. Everything, there would be no end to it . . . A wave crisped over. It was cold enough, now, to freeze the sea.

He left the beach.

Tonight, they had drawn the curtains, he could not see who was in there. But he had made up his mind, he would not be afraid now. He thought, I can do anything.

Voices and light and smoke were like a pod bursting open, as he pushed on the door. They had all looked up from their tables, over by the fire, expecting someone else. The door closed with a sucking sound at Duncan's back. They were silent, they might all have been struck dumb. Duncan felt his head begin to sing. He all but turned and ran out, as he had always run, to hide somewhere in the darkness far off, by the tower or in the old boat on the river, he waited for them all to stand up and come over towards him, to be blamed and then beaten, for their huge bodies to block out the light, the fear spurted like water through his belly.

Nothing. Silence.

In the end, someone said, "What's happened to Bert Malt tonight, then?" into the room, so that the spell was broken and they all came alive again, turning their heads away from Duncan, starting to drink.

He had not known what it would smell or sound like in here, he had been nowhere like it before. He realized that they were not going to touch him.

The woman behind the bar said, "Old enough are you?" and laughed, her soft pink face opening about her soft pink mouth, though she knew who he was and how old, knew, as they all did, everything about him.

He put his hand down into his pocket, fumbling about for the money he had, a florin and a sixpence.

"I suppose you've come for change. Change or a box of matches!"

He saw that the flesh of her hands was soft, too, and thick all the way down each finger, it was as if she had no bones, everything was soft and slack. "Is it matches? Has your mother written it down for you?" She leaned forward, speaking to him loudly.

Duncan said, "I want a drink."

"It's our Duncan!"

He stiffened. John Dent from the builder's yard had come across, and stood in front of him, John Dent with the dark, ferrety face, balancing backwards and forwards on the balls of his feet.

"Taken to drink, have you?"

Duncan shook his head anxiously.

"All right, then, I'll buy you something, young Duncan, I'll pay for your drink." John Dent was laughing, his eyes and teeth shining like the pebbles under frost.

"Give our Duncan what he wants, then. What do you want?"

Feverishly, Duncan pulled his hand out of his pocket and dropped the two coins on to the counter. "I've got enough money, I've enough to pay."

"What if you have? I've told you, I'll pay for you, and watch you drink it. Whatever you want. All right? What's the matter?"

Duncan wanted to cry with frustration, for he would have accepted and drunk, that was how things were and it was easy, and he could not do it, did not know what to say and did not trust John Dent.

"You've got to speak up in here, our Duncan, you'll get nowhere like that, will you?"

"Leave him," she said. "He can't help it, he doesn't know what you're on about."

John Dent was smiling, not minding her.

"Pull him a pint of bitter."

"What is it you want, now? John's buying you your drink, you put your money away. What is it you'd like?"

In the end, because he could not answer, she did as John Dent said, gave him beer, and he took out money and paid her.

"Put your own back in your pocket, Duncan Pike, buy yourself some sweeties."

He wandered away, back to his table, losing interest. But looking back to the bar, he saw Duncan's thin throat swallowing down the beer, and felt full of malice, wondered what else he might do. Dafty-Duncan.

He had never drunk beer before, but he scarcely tasted it now, he was so thirsty after painting the garden benches, he drank it like water, without a pause.

"I can pay for it with my money," he said stubbornly, "I should pay."

"It's been paid for." She spoke sharply to him, not wanting him to stay there, so close to the bar. But he left all of the money on the counter, beside the empty glass and as he went out, he could hear the silence in which they waited to talk about him. John Dent's eyes were steady, green as grass, on his back.

He caught his breath as the outside air hit his face, and he was shaking with reaction from what he had done. Along Tide Street, he wondered why he had wanted to go there, and everything in his head began to tumble about, the pictures were there again.

They lost interest shortly, and stopped talking about Duncan Pike, went back to the lifeboat disaster and the splendour of that morning's funeral. The barmaid took Duncan's money and tipped it into the till.

All that evening, he sat by the fire, staring down into the pear logs, the skin of his face burning, and her voice bored its way on and on, through the pictures in his head.

"What do you think I am — Do you think I can't tell? I wasn't born yesterday, Duncan Pike. I've waited for it, waited for anything, I wouldn't put anything past you. And if you start drinking, do you know where it's going to end? No, you do not, you wouldn't be able to see. And where are you going to get the money? They'll not buy it for you, they're not your friends. You don't have anything to do with them, I've told you. Like that Ted Flint, coming here, looking like he did — what right had he got?"

His lips felt thick and numb inside, as though the blood was thawing out.

"That's what you'll turn out like, that Ted Flint. He's nothing, just nothing. I've told you about things often enough, I've told you the way you are. This world wasn't designed for people like you, Duncan Pike, your face doesn't fit. And now you come in here smelling of drink, and what else? You start drinking and you'll lose that job, such as it is, that's something sure, they'll not have you up there any dafter than you are now. So you'll live off me, I shall have to keep you, you'll be idle and thriftless, and where will all of it end? You listen to me, boy, I'm telling you the truth, I'm telling you what's for your own good, nothing more. We're nothing to any of them, do you understand me? We could be dead and buried and there'd be no processions at our funeral. We're nothing. I know. I came here, didn't I, I brought you up — don't you tell me."

Though he had said nothing to her. When he came in, he had found her beside the fire, and he did not ask who had brought her home from the empty church.

In the kitchen he had prepared their supper, doing what she told him, frying eggs and toasting bread, and his eyes had filmed over, his face felt swollen, after the drink of beer. And she had talked and talked, the same things over again, like a chant, the tone of her voice never altering, and her fingers flicking in and out of the white crochet. He was no longer anxious, he felt a new person, strong, by himself.

The fire burned furiously, piled high with logs, so that the tiny room was stifling hot, the polished surfaces of the furniture were scorched. He sat on the leather stool, hypnotized by the fire, waiting. He scarcely heard anything of what his mother said, though he looked up from time to time, and saw her, the high, white forehead under the scraped-back hair, and the white mouth moving, the fingers clasped around the steel hook.

"You're mad! Look at that fire. Where do we get more wood from when that's all done? You don't go asking for any more. What are you trying to do, burn the house down?"

He hunched himself up more closely, and fed another thin log into the fire, excited by its quick burning. He could smell the soot, carried in clots, sparking, up the chimney.

"You go on like this and they'll put you away, I'll ask them, I will. And then what? You're not fit to be out, the things you do, but what'll happen to me? You don't think of that. You won't listen, won't try, will you?"

But in the end, the crochet square was finished, she cut the wool and told him that she would go to bed. The fire was dying down a little, thick with ash.

"You needn't take all night, getting ready," Hilda Pike said.

He went into the icy back kitchen and switched on the light. He filled the kettle and waited for it to boil and put the pan of milk on the back stove to warm and got down her blue mug. He took the brown bottle of capsules out of the cupboard and tipped a dozen into his hand, took the cap off the end of each one and poured the powder out, into the bottom of the milk mug. The husks of the capsules were clear turquoise, like cellophane in the palm of his hand. He held one up to his eye and lifted his head up to the light, and the kitchen was reflected blue to him, as though he were under water. The kettle boiled, and then the pan of milk.

She said, "You watch that fire. You put it down properly before you go to bed."

Duncan picked her up out of the wheelchair, not speaking. He realized that he must think of everything he had to do, because it was never easy, he might forget anything, the way he was.

After he had settled her and closed the bedroom door, he came downstairs and simply waited, on the leather stool beside the fire. He felt as though he had stepped outside of himself. There was everything to see, a whole world, down inside the flickering fire.

It was half-past two when he stirred. The logs had all been used up, though the last was still burning. He stumbled to his feet, cramped, and went out through the kitchen to fetch an armful more. The gutters were all frozen over, icicles hanging in a clear smooth stream down from the backyard tap.

He rebuilt the fire, raking out all the old flakes of ash and cinder, and making a bed of kindling, criss-crossing the pear logs one on top of the other and then holding the first match steadily, blowing a little, to make a draught. The grate was still hot. When the fire was alight again, he went upstairs.

She was strangely heavy, dead or asleep, he could not tell which. He dressed her again and pushed back her hair into the metal comb, and carried her downstairs. He put on the coat that she had worn for the funeral, the hat and gloves.

Outside, nothing moved, it was as though the world had been bound by ice and frost and only he was free and alive, pushing the wheelchair along the glistening street. Out on the path, beside the sea wall, the cold was like a solid block through which he had to pass. He thought the skin of his face would peel off. The sky was quite clear, arching over the sea and the marshes and pricking with stars. The wheels of the chair slid smoothly along the path, making no sound.

Duncan thought of nothing, felt nothing. He had decided what he should do and could not remember a reason.

A little way beyond the martello tower, the wall jutted out as a breakwater, like a finger pointing into the sea. He walked to the very end, and then stopped, and went forward, to look down through the darkness. The stones were very slippery. Below him, the sea moved, the tide was high up at the top of the beach. Here it was very glassy, very deep, the beach shelved down steeply so that even at low tide, this end of the jetty was surrounded by it.

Duncan hesitated, waiting. A wave built up, stirring the surface of the water, rising as it moved up towards the shingle. It lifted and tipped over, and as it came down, he pushed the wheelchair gently forward. It slipped at once, over the edge and out of sight, and the noise was lost in the suck and hiss of the waves. He had not wanted to hear anything.

Duncan put his hands in his pockets and began to

walk very quickly away, watching his feet over the black ice. By the martello, he looked up. The sea had started to shine queerly with phosphor, like cold fire. To his left, the marshes creaked with frost, the hidden birds completely still. He ran harder, ducking his head.

The fire was burning high again in the grate. He bent down and pressed two more logs on to it.

At first, he was going to pile up as much as he could on the wheelbarrow and take it down to the beach, he could burn it there. He had not thought, until now, that the tide was high, and that in any case he would be seen, the bonfire would be a beacon for miles up the coast, and for the whole town of Heype. So, he must burn everything here in the grate of the dark front room. He went about the house, choosing what he hated most and what would most easily burn, pulling down curtains and stripping the covers off cushions. He took the bag full of completed crochet and fed the squares and circles into the flames. Then he went upstairs to fetch bedding and clothes, and into the kitchen for scissors.

It was the hardest work he had ever done, it took a long time, cutting and tearing and burning and raking out. At first, the sight of the flames excited him, but later, he stumbled a little, through each room, as if he did not know his way about. He would have burned the terrible furniture but he could think of no way, it defeated him now, as it had always defeated him.

He heard sounds first, out in the street, the clatter of milk crates and the roar of lorries, and then, later, the light, easing into the room through the curtainless windows, dulling the fire.

He took nothing with him. The most important thing of all seemed that he should be by himself, the old life piled up behind him anyhow, discarded. When he left the house, he wore only the clothes he always worked in, and his woollen jacket and Wellington boots. From the drawer in the oak dresser, he took four pound notes and some coins, all the money there was. He locked the front door.

The marshes were empty and beautiful. At his back, the sun was silver-white, over the sea. He began to walk along the river bank. The reeds and clumps of grass were frosted over, so that each blade was separated thinly from the rest, and the petalled leaves of clover and meadow-moss were stiff and dust-white, like flowers upon an iced cake. Under the banks the still river was marbled, like frozen phlegm.

Where the old boat was, the river curved away through the marshes, inland. Duncan followed it, for nearly six miles, without pausing, his legs moving rhythmically like the pumps of a machine. Under the woollen coat and jumper, his body began to sweat. His head had gone quiet and his mind was blank as the sky, he remembered nothing, the pictures were all gone, the voices silent.

Eventually, the river narrowed and ran under a low stone bridge. He stopped. Just ahead of him, the roofs of houses, the village of Iyde, flint-grey under the sun. The marshes led away into fields, rutted with snow.

Duncan turned round and looked back, and terror broke through him, at the brightness of everything, the openness of the land and the river and marsh, the endless clear sky, he felt himself standing upright, thin and dark in the midst of it. The sun glittered on the snow, and reflected up through his eyes and ears and nostrils, into his head, where it began to burn, and to make a strange noise, thin and high and clear as metal.

The river went under the bridge and through a field to his left. Then it broadened out again. There was a disused mill, and a low, slate-roofed grain-barn, and when he saw them, he remembered the time he had come here before, he had run away from school and walked. But then it had grown dark and he went inside the barn. A long time afterwards, they had found him.

His legs felt brittle as he moved again, and his arms, too, bent in at his sides. A marsh hare fled across the path in front of him. Nothing else moved except, now and then, the river, as it began to thaw slightly under the sun.

The door of the barn was swinging open on its hinges. Inside it was very cold and dry, but with a faint, musty smell, as though once something had rotted here, in water. Light came through wooden slats at the windows, in lines like gold wires lying across the floor. At the far end, a short wooden staircase with a handrail led up into the roof, and here there was a little more light. The wooden floor was bone-dry, and still scattered with old grain and bits of husk.

The pile of sacks he remembered was still there, in the corner, nobody had moved anything in the years since he had hidden here, nobody came to this place. He lay down, drawing his knees up to his chest. He felt safe, dark. So this was where he had wanted to be, then. This place. He felt no surprise.

By mid-morning, the smoke and flames from the cottage in Tide Street had begun to pour out of windows and chimney, around the cracks in the front door.

At the Big House, Cragg waited in evil temper until ten past ten, and then went down in search of him, wanting the garden benches to be finished that day.

A crowd gathered, word had reached the top of the town, and then the men axed their way inside, expecting to find Hilda Pike, trapped in her wheelchair, but finding only the furniture burning ferociously, the old wood dust-dry.

From three miles out, Davey Ward stood up in his boat and saw the rising plume of smoke. The sun was dazzling bright on the skin of the sea. He turned and went on, further out towards the sandbanks to fish.

At Walwick, the body of Hilda Pike came ashore with the tide, and later, higher up the coast, the empty wheelchair.

When they found Duncan, and led him out of the grain-barn, he pulled the collar of his jacket up, trying to keep the light out of his face. As they drove away, the engine of the car began to make a noise through his head, like singing. They did not take him back to Heype.

The frost held hard for a week, and up at the Big House, Cragg finished the painting of the garden benches, and chopped the last of the logs, and at twelve-fifteen, went into the toolshed to read through the newspaper and eat his lunch alone.

The metal hair comb was found, as it lay caught and glinting between two pebbles on the beach, out beyond the martello. Old Beattie fingered it for a moment, and then dropped it into the old pram and went on, keeping close to the edge of the water.

Later that day, the wind veered west, blowing in soft-bellied rainclouds. The thaw began.

The Elephant Man

It was on the same day that they drained the Round Pond, for the first time in forty years, that Nanny Fawcett met her Friend. And in all the time the three of them spent together afterwards, she never gave him any name in front of the child, he was always My Friend.

William had asked anxiously about the Pond, what it would look like, how big it would be now?

"The same size as always, won't it? *That's* a silly question."

"Just with no water in it?"

"We don't say 'with no' we say 'without any'."

"Yes. How big will the pit be?"

"What pit? There won't be any *pit*, will there? Lift your arms up."

The stream of lather came trickling around both sides of his neck and down his pale chest. At the edges of the bath, the scum was grey, when the water moved. He struggled to imagine the Round Pond, to which he went every day, empty of its expanse of water, rippled across the centre by the wind, but he failed, he could not picture it and was alarmed by his ignorance of how it might be.

"If there won't be a pit, what *will* there be, then?"

A grip fell down into the bath out of Nanny Fawcett's coiled-up red hair, as she bent over him.

"Mud," she said sharply. "Stand up." There was a

line of sweat-beads along her upper lip. She retrieved the grip impatiently. Wary of her moods, which came unpredictably, and then hung about her, thickening and tainting the atmosphere of rooms, he did not ask what would have happened to the ducks. He imagined them, kept in individual, waterless cages, and fed by keepers with broken bread, and later, hung in rows by their webbed, pink feet along the steel rail at Murchison's, Butcher and Poulterer.

Nanny Fawcett began to rub him with a very dry towel.

At the beginning, there had been another Nanny, about whom he now remembered only a smell, and an air of weariness and loss of hope. "I was trained in the old school," she had said, on arrival, "I am only used to the best type of home." And she had been firm in her demands for Sole Charge and no sweets of any kind and the sacking of the cleaning woman who used bad language. "But then she is so reliable and decided," William's mother had said, sipping a Manhattan in the oyster-grey drawing-room, "everything is so nice for me, so straightforward." Though, in truth, she felt a little guilty that this was so, believed obscurely that it was not altogether natural to have a nanny who gave simply no trouble. So that it had been almost a salve to her conscience when that Nanny had, abruptly, died, and the problems of finding someone new and suitable began. William was three and a half.

He could not now imagine how it had been before Nanny Fawcett came to the house, he saw the world entirely through her eyes, all his experience of life reached him filtered through her. Nanny Fawcett was Irish, she was in her middle thirties, she came from a good, Protestant family in Dublin, she was moody. Her breasts were too large and concealed a heart filled with prejudice, most markedly against men, and against the Republic of Eire.

William's mother had some weeks of anxiety. "I do hope we have done the right thing, she did *seem* the most suitable, though it is clear to us all that Nannies are not what they were. But I am afraid that I suspect Nanny Fawcett of dying her hair. That red is so unnatural." She spoke as one of some distant generation, but she was not old-fashioned, merely true to her breeding. She spoke in a high-pitched, nasal, slightly whining voice. But she felt, too, a little more comfortable with Nanny Fawcett, felt secure in her own position as mistress of both house and child. It was only what one expected, to have to put up with some quirks, in a Nanny.

When they visited the house in Cadogan Square, William's maternal grandmother sat among the fringed sofas from Peter Jones, the skin beneath her eyes most carefully powdered, and asked, "What about this Nanny Fawcett?" "But I think, you know," said William's mother, when they had discussed it, "that she is *all right*, I think that everything is as it should be, on the whole. Of course, I would never entrust William to just anybody."

They could feel their duty done, then, and dismiss the child's welfare under Nanny Fawcett from their minds.

To William, the only realities of which he could be certain, the only truths he knew, came to him through

Nanny Fawcett. Everywhere else was the territory of strangers, the ground upon which he walked, in company with his mother and father and the Cadogan Square grandmother, was insubstantial. He sensed that he could never have survived, permanently, in their atmosphere. From Nanny Fawcett he learned that there were "Irish *and* Irish", and that the Protestants of good family living in Dublin kept themselves very much to themselves, they had their own clubs and dances and private schools.

"A trained Nanny," she said, over and over again, "is not a servant. This is a profession. I am not a *maid*, you know, nothing of that kind."

He learned about the spoliation of Dublin's Georgian buildings and about the low character of the feckless Southern Irish, Roman Catholics and working class, who came over to England and gave their country a bad name. He learned about the winning ways and loose morals of the colleens who worked as waitresses in Lyons Corner House and conductresses on buses of the Green Line. He learned about the integrity of the Unionist party and the reign of terror by bigoted priests among the peasants of Eire. He learned that Nanny Fawcett's grandmother bred Irish setter dogs, and that her family had always been "proud". Above all, he learned that most of the trouble in the world, and all the troubles of women, could be laid at the door of men.

"You'll be a man," she said, laying his checked Viyella shirt out on the chair. "You'll be as bad as all the rest." And he had felt suddenly ashamed, knowing that his days were strictly numbered with her. He wished that he might do something to change his sex, to grow up or in some other way escape from the general mantle of male guilt. He was uncertain how he stood with Nanny Fawcett, what she truly thought of him. Her eyes, upturned slightly at the corners like those of an Oriental, flitted over him and gave him no reassurance, nothing more than a casual, spasmodic approval for some point of manners remembered or temptation not succumbed to. He planned ways to ingratiate himself with her, so that he might perceive some definite sign that her commendation would last for ever. But always, the eyes swept quickly over him, and he despaired. There was only the immediate chance of an hour, or day, of favour to cling to, he learned to live his life in these small snatches. They were like stepping stones, below which ran the dark river of her moods.

And so, he was surprised, the first day they met the Friend. It was January, slate-grey, a cold wind cutting across between the trees at their legs. He began to trail behind Nanny Fawcett up the slope, anxious about how the Round Pond would look, of how he might cope with getting to know it all over again, the unfamiliar.

"Don't scrape your shoes, you've only just this week had a new pair."

Today, her hair shone redder than before, and the coils were more elaborate, gripped under the navy-blue hat. She had said, "You're to behave yourself very nicely and not to be a nuisance, you're to make a good impression."

"Why?"

"Because we might be going to meet someone, that's

why. And you're having a jumper on under that coat, the wind's enough to cut you in half."

He wondered who it was that they might see, if it was not the other Nannies, beside whom she would sometimes sit, on the green bench. Though, more often than not, she ignored them, neither sat nor talked, preferring to keep herself apart. The others, she had told him, had nothing of interest to say, or else they gave themselves airs, or were in charge of unsuitable children.

"Who might we see?"

"Never you mind, you'll find out in good time — and that's something else, you're to be quiet and not to go pestering with questions like you do, and 'I want this, I want that', every five minutes. We want a bit of peace and quiet to ourselves, my friend and I."

He gave up trying to imagine what kind of friend Nanny Fawcett might have. At the top of the slope, he walked forwards a little, and then stopped. The Pond was huge, it had spread and spread, with the exit of the water it seemed to him that he would never be able to walk as far as the opposite edge, he could barely see it. It was mud, thick and stiff and sculptured into lines of thin waves, towards the rim, as though the water had coagulated. He noticed the boats, beached on the mud and larded with it, so that their shape was disguised. They had been there for years, he thought, since before he was born, they had been there forever.

"Don't stand staring at that, it's only a basinful of mud, and thick with germs, I shouldn't wonder, there's nothing to see."

But he could not take his eyes off the landscape of

the pond, the craters and pits, the branches of trees and the abandoned boats picked out on it, he wanted to step down and walk across, poking and digging, to get into the centre where no one could reach him, not even the men with long grappling hooks, who sometimes had to bring the boats in, when the wind dropped.

Nanny Fawcett caught his hand. "Did you *hear* me?" He went after her, away from the Pond and up towards the bandstand on the edge of the trees.

For a long time, nobody came. He went away from her and down between the horse-chestnut trees, mashing the old leaves with his feet. He found an almost straight stick and held it like a lance. No other children were here, only, some yards away, a woman in green with a dog. From the beginning the afternoon had been strangely different, this place was not like the gardens to which he usually came, to rush about and sail a boat, while Nanny Fawcett looked on. The whole landscape was changed, everything was coloured differently, and the trees were a new shape. The Pond was dry. They might have been in another country. He was excited by it, and a little alarmed.

From far away, down the pleached walk came the shouts of boys, high and thin in the wind. He began to poke about in the leaves again with his straight stick.

When he looked up, he saw that Nanny Fawcett's friend had arrived, they were sitting together beside the empty bandstand. Nanny Fawcett touched her hand now and again to the coils of hair underneath the navy-blue hat. After a moment or two, William went nearer. The fact that her friend was a man completed his sense of strangeness, everything was suddenly out of joint in his view of the world and of people, if Nanny Fawcett, who despised men, could be so publicly friendly with one, nodding and smiling on the green bench.

He looked, William thought, as though his clothes did not belong to him, as though he were used to wearing something quite different. Though they were ordinary, a grey tweed overcoat, rather long, over grey trousers, and an egg-yellow scarf. And his face, the shape of his head and the set of his flesh across the bones, seemed not to fit with the rest of him, he was like a figure out of the Crazy Men game, where you moved a row of heads along, fitting them in turn to a row of different bodies underneath, and none of them seemed exactly to belong. Something in the man's features was constantly changing, as though he were trying on new expressions, toying with them and then discarding them, he smiled and grimaced and frowned and formed his mouth into a little, soft, pursed shape, and the flesh of his forehead slipped up and down somehow, under the shelf of thinning hair, the skin of his neck was loose.

William thought that he was old — and then not so old, it was hard to tell. He had a lot of very long teeth, and a tiny chin, and very pale, gloveless hands.

He moved the stick about on the grass at his feet, and Nanny Fawcett saw him.

"Come here now, you're not to go off too far into those trees by yourself — come right here. This is him, this is William — stand up properly, child — Now, *here* is the person I told you we might be going to meet." She was talking much faster than usual, and every now and then, her hand went up to the coils of hair. William took a step nearer the bench, and the man leaned down and put out one of the pale hands, smiling with all his teeth, as though it were a joke, that they should be so formally introduced. William thought, he is not a very old man, but he is older than my father. He said, "They've emptied the water out of the Round Pond. It's just mud now."

"Ah!" said Nanny Fawcett's friend, and the expression on his face slipped and changed again, and now he looked secretive, he put a tongue inside his cheek and made it swell out a little, as though he were sucking a toffee. "I daresay you wanted to sail a boat, didn't you? I daresay that's the trouble."

"No, I didn't, I like it empty. I want it to stay like that. There are boats that have sunk, you can see them. And twigs. There are . . ."

"Off you go," Nanny Fawcett said, suddenly impatient. "Don't chatter so, about nothing, off you go and run about and don't wander too far off into those trees, do you hear me?"

He saw her turn a little on the bench, so that she was facing the Friend, saw a bright expression come into her face, as though everything he had said and would say were all that could interest her. The man turned his back, so that there was only the dark grey tweed and the line of yellow scarf below.

William moved away, chilled by the abrupt loss of their attention, and wandered about on the path by the trees. His hands were cold inside the woollen gloves. He wanted something to happen, for the day to become familiar again. Above his head, and stretching away into the distance, the sky was uniformly pale, and grey as brains. The woman in green, with the dog, had gone, everybody was going, out of the January wind.

Under one of the horse-chestnuts he found a conker, and although the green pulpy case had blemished, and the spines were soft and rotten, inside the nut was perfect, hard and polished like a mahogany table. He scooped it out and held it, feeling it slip, shiny, between his fingers. When he disturbed the leaves, the soil and moss beneath the trees sent up a cold, sweet stench.

He heard nothing, only saw the feet and legs in front of him. Very slowly he straightened up, holding the stick. It was another man. William glanced over to Nanny Fawcett, sitting with her friend on the park bench, wanting reassurance. Their faces were turned away from him.

"Nice," the man said, "that's nice." His eyes were sharp and vacant at the same time, and he had a tall head. William stepped back.

"I could give you another. I could give you a lot." And suddenly his hand shot out from under the mackintosh, and in the open palm lay eight or nine conkers, huge and glossy. "I might give them all to you."

"That's all right, I've got my own, thank you," William was afraid of not being polite enough to the man, touched by the offer of the conkers, yet uneasy, not liking him to be there. When he looked again, the conkers had disappeared, and so had the man's hand, back into the pocket of the raincoat, so that he wondered whether he had seen them or not, and the man stood, smiling at him. The collar of his shirt was stiff, and shiny white.

"What's your name?"

"William."

"That's nice. That's what I like."

A gust of wind came knifing through the trees, stirring the dead leaves, and rattling down a loose branch. Abruptly, the man turned and began to move away, slipping round the grey trunks until he had vanished as quickly as the conkers had vanished. William stood, remembering the way he had come there. He dropped the conker into his coat pocket and kept his fingers tightly round it.

"Men," Nanny Fawcett had said. "There's always something that's not right about men, always something." Now, he felt betrayed somehow, left alone among the trees with a stranger who offered him conkers, while she went on talking to her new friend.

On the way home, he asked if they would see him again.

"Oh, now, that all depends and don't little boys ask a lot of questions?"

They were walking very quickly, everyone was leaving the gardens and going off down the concrete slopes to tea, it was too cold for snow, she said, and he was out of breath now, with trying to keep up to her.

"But we might, and then again we might not, there might be treats in store, we might be seeing him somewhere else."

"Where else? What sort of place?"

No answer.

"Doesn't he go to work?"

Nanny Fawcett rounded upon him alarmingly. "Of course he goes to work, don't all honest men go to work, what do you take me for? I wouldn't have anything to do with any layabout, any idle man, you needn't imagine that I would."

"No," William said.

"But if we were to go and see him at work — well now, we might and that would be something!"

"What does he do?"

"Oh, something that would just surprise you." Nanny Fawcett gripped his hand as they crossed the road at Kensington Gore. "Something you'll never have heard of, and never would expect."

"Tell me about it, *tell* me."

"You'll find out soon enough, I daresay you will find out."

Her face was flushed, set against the wind, and he dared not ask now, how her friend was different from all the rest, how he managed to escape her blanket condemnation of men. He had not looked any different. But perhaps he might learn the trick from him, if they met again, perhaps he could listen and watch, and discover the secret of Nanny Fawcett's favour.

He had tea in the oyster-grey drawing-room, with an apricot Danish pastry brought in by his grandmother from Cadogan Square.

"We're not going to the Park today, we're going somewhere different. It's to be a treat."

He was being dressed in best trousers and a white shirt, his mother had gone out. "Mum's the word,"

Nanny Fawcett had said. He wondered what to expect, dared not ask.

Outside a hotel, they stopped. Nanny Fawcett bent down to him. "You're to enjoy yourself," she said, pumping his hand up and down to emphasize her words. "You're not to be a trouble. You go with my friend and do as you're told, and remember just how lucky you are."

He looked up at her, prepared for anything at all. Nanny Fawcett laughed. "Cow's eyes!" she said. "You'll be the death of me. It's a *party*, isn't it?"

They walked up the wide, white marble steps of the hotel and through the revolving doors, and inside everything was hushed and softly lit from chandeliers, the carpets were rose-red on the floor. Nanny Fawcett held hard on to his hand. It was some minutes before her friend came, looking more than ever strange, in shirt sleeves, and with his hair combed flat back, as though he had been disturbed from a sleep, or in the middle of some job, up a ladder. William wondered if he lived in the hotel. He made a curious face at him, screwing the flesh up around his eyes and nose, and then letting it collapse again like a pile of ash, looking blandly at Nanny Fawcett.

"Well," he said. "It's all fixed up, you see, all arranged."

"I wouldn't like to think that it was not," said Nanny Fawcett.

He brayed with laughter, showing the long teeth.

"*We* were not coming to the back entrance," Nanny Fawcett said.

The friend's hand shot out and pinched William's cheek, and he danced a little, on the balls of his feet.

"Time presses," he said. "We'll do well to be getting off, getting this one settled and so forth. Well, now . . ." He winked.

"Get *along* . . ." Nanny Fawcett gave him a little push in the back, "and you mind your manners, I'll be around to collect you later, won't I?"

The friend waved his arm in the direction of a deserted lounge, full of green and gold armchairs. "What about getting settled," he said, "having a nice tray of tea, what about you going and putting your feet up, and I'll be down directly."

He took William's hand.

He had thought that the upstairs corridors of hotels led only to bedrooms, but when they emerged from the left, there were tall cream-painted pillars, and huge, fronded plants, and gilt mirrors, and they walked towards another lounge.

"Going to enjoy yourself?" the friend said.

William frowned.

"Well, don't have a lot to say, do you? Don't have much of a tongue in your head."

He leered down horribly, the rubber face contorting itself and seeming to flush and darken, until a grin broke it open like a wave, and everything was different again. William wondered if the face changed in sleep, too.

"Where am I going?"

They stopped. The friend banged him lightly on the

back. "Well, to a *party*, aren't you? You're going to a party."

"Oh. Is it your party?"

"It is not."

A door swung open ahead, letting out voices.

"All you've to do, you've to mind what you say, then you'll be nice and dandy, you see, and nothing to do but enjoy yourself."

He did not explain further.

At Christmas, there had been four parties, and none of them was at a hotel and all of them had terrified him, each time he had prayed that there would never be another. Now, he stood back behind Nanny Fawcett's friend, looking upon the room full of strangers, other children, in ribbon and net and velvet and white shirts under tartan ties, and his stomach clenched with dread. He did not know why he had been brought here.

"Well now, how very nice!" said the woman in mauve, bending down to him, "How nice, dear! We were expecting you." And she turned to the other, beside her. "Our entertainer's child!" she said, and both of them laughed a little, and looked about the room for someone to take charge of him. "His name is William," she said.

He had thought that always one met the same people at parties, his cousin Sophie and the Cressett twins and fat Michael, but he knew nobody here at all, their names confused him and he hung back on the edge of their games.

"We've been told to be nice to you," a boy said.

William stood, thinking of Nanny Fawcett and the

friend, far away down all the carpeted stairs, eating tea in the empty lounge.

As it went on, it became like all the other parties he had known, the terrors were at least familiar, the awful taste of the tea and of trifles in little, waxed paper cases and the staring of the bigger girls. There were games which he did not win and dancing for which he had not brought his pumps. The woman in mauve clapped her hands and laughed a lot and changed the records on the gramophone, and from time to time, she took his hand and led him closer into the circle of the others. "You are to look after this little boy, you are to be kind to William now, dear, try and remember."

But then, suddenly, one of the hotel waiters had drawn the curtains and they were all made to sit tightly together on the carpeted floor, squealing a little with apprehension and excitement. Then the music began. Oh God, Oh God, make it not be a a conjuror or a Punch and Judy, William thought, pressing his nails deeply into the palms of his hands. But it was not, it was something he had never seen before, something worse.

The area ahead of them was lit like a stage, with a high stool placed there, and then a figure came lumbering out of the darkness. From the shoulders down it was a man, his costume all in one piece and wumbling as it moved, like the covering on a pantomime horse. But it stood upon only two legs and the legs were three times, ten times, as long as human legs, and oddly stiff at the joints. Above the shoulders, the huge head was not a man's head, but that of an elephant, nodding and bobbing and bending forward to the music and waving its disgusting trunk.

William sat and every so often closed his eyes, willing for it to be gone, for the curtains to be drawn again and the ordinary January daylight to flood the room. But he could still hear the music and when that stopped, the elephant man spoke and sang, the voice very deep, distorted and hollow, booming away inside the huge head. He opened his eyes and did not want to look, but he could not stop himself, the square of light and then the lurching animal man drew him. It was dancing, lifting its huge legs up and down stiffly, clapping its hands together, while the head nodded. From somewhere, it produced a vividly coloured stuffed parrot, which sat upon its shoulder and answered back to jokes, in a terrible rasping voice. Then the music started again.

"Now, children, now what about everybody doing a little dance with me, what about us all dancing together? Would you like that?"

"Yes," they yelled. "Yes, Yes!" and clapped and bounced up and down.

"And what about somebody coming up on my shoulder and being as high as the sky, what about that? Would you like to do that?"

"Yes," they screamed. "Yes, yes!" and rushed forwards, clamouring about the baggy legs, clutching and laughing.

From the gramophone came the music for a Conga, and the elephant man set off with everyone clinging on behind in a chain, prancing about the room, and first one, then another was lifted high up on to its great shoulders, swaying with delight, hands touching the ceiling, swinging the chandelier. William stood back against the wall in the darkness, praying not to be noticed, but when the line reached him, he was noticed, the woman in mauve clucked and took his hand, putting him in with the others, so that he was forced to trot on one leg and then the next to the music. And then, suddenly, he felt the elephant man behind him, and he was lifted up, the hands digging tightly into his sides, and he could neither scream nor protest, he could scarcely breathe, only dangle helplessly there, near to the cream-painted ceiling, and see, far below him, the upturned, mocking faces of the others, hear the blast of the music. Through the slits in the elephant head, he could see eyes, flickering like lanterns in a turnip, and he looked away dizzy, praying to be set down.

At the end, the lights did not go on immediately, he could slip out of the door and nobody noticed him.

The corridor was silent, everything closed and secret. The music faded away as he ran, and found a flight of stairs and climbed them, not daring to look back. Here the passages were narrower, the carpets dark grey and thick as felt, so that his feet made no sound. There might have been nobody else in the building.

He had thought that he would die of fear, high up in the clutch of the elephant man, but he had not died, and now he must remember it, he could still hear the music and the shrieking of the others, pounding in his ears. He came up to a long mirror at the end of the corridor, and was terrified by his own reflection, tense and white-faced. The elephant man could be following him, might be anywhere at all, and perhaps there were others. He began to run, back down the stairs, but on the lower corridor heard voices and imagined some punishment inflicted upon him by the elephant man, or else by the hotel porters and maids, and the woman in mauve. He pushed open one of the grey doors in his panic. When the voices and footsteps had gone away, he would run again down to the lounge where Nanny Fawcett was having tea with her friend, it would be all right.

"Well, now!"

He spun round. It was a bedroom, with draped curtains and a light switched on over the long dressing-table, and reflected in the mirror, he saw the elephant man, arms up on either side of his head. He could not move, only stare in terror as the hands lifted off the grey head, up and up, and then down again, until it rested on his knees.

"Master William the party-boy," said Nanny Fawcett's friend, and the face creased in sudden, wicked mirth, trembling and quivering. On a chair, William saw Nanny Fawcett's navy-blue coat and hat, and the sensible handbag. "All a bit of a romp and a treat," said her friend, "blowed if it isn't!" His face crumpled into sadness and mock-weeping. "Poor old elephant!"

William saw the two images separately, the face of the man, and that of the elephant on his lap, and then the reflections of them in the glass, he was surrounded by the terrible faces. He gave a sob, and put up a hand to shield his eyes, groping for the door-handle. It would not yield, something pushed him back, and then there was Nanny Fawcett, straightening her skirt, he was forced to go back into the room, while her friend the elephant man laughed until the tears ran down his cheeks. Outside in the corridor, the voices of the others, leaving the party.

"You didn't collect your present," Nanny Fawcett said.

Because it was raining and the hotel was not near home, they went on a bus.

"You never would have guessed it, I know, never in a million years," Nanny Fawcett said, her face flushed with pleasure. "He used to be in the pantomimes and circuses, my friend, he's a very high class entertainer."

The lights of the cars swept down Piccadilly in a row, like an army advancing through the rain.

"You're the lucky one, aren't you, there's plenty that would envy you, I know. Going to a party and not even knowing the person! Well!"

He realized that he had not discovered for which child the party had been held.

"You've gone quiet," she said, making him walk too quickly round the Square. "If you ate too much, I shan't be very pleased, shall I, after what I told you?"

He thought of the dreams he would have that night.

"Mum's the word," Nanny Fawcett said, turning her key in the latch. For he must say nothing about her friend and nothing about the party.

He woke in the darkness to find his pillow, and the well of the bed below his neck, filled with vomit.

"The *next* time, you learn to hold back," said Nanny Fawcett, stripping off his pyjamas. Her hair was twisted into curious plaits about her head. "Your eyes are bigger than your stomach, so they are. The next time you just curb your greed, thank you very much."

He stared into her face, and did not dare ask about "the next time". "He's a very nice type of man," she said, rubbing the cold sponge briskly about his face. "Not at all the sort you would commonly meet, so mind your P's and Q's in future and play your cards right and you'll be going to quite a number of parties, I shouldn't wonder."

Lying in the dark again, between stiff, clean sheets, he knew that since the day they drained the Round Pond, everything had surely changed and would never be as it was, and felt afraid, wishing for the time past, when Nanny Fawcett had despised all men.

Friends of Miss Reece

"You're in the way," Wetherby said, but quietly, hissing under her breath, in case Matron, who was also the boy's Aunt, should come in through the door.

"Nuisance . . . as if there weren't enough."

She bent down and jabbed at the coals with a black poker, so that they burst hotly open like poppy pods, showering sparks for seeds. He watched her covertly, out of the sides of his eyes, feeling ashamed of being so disliked. The warmth from the fire came up into his face.

"You can drink your milk on the hearth stool, you won't get under everyone's feet," his Aunt Spencer had said. But she was kind, beneath the sharp way of talking. He had always known her.

"*Which* room was I born in?"

"Number Six, next to the old nursery, down the corridor from Reece."

It was familiar as a rhyme. When he asked, she answered, automatically, banging in and out of the swing doors with trays and pans and white enamel jugs of steaming water, always using the same words.

"Number Six, next to the old nursery, down the corridor from Reece."

It was his mother who refused to comfort him in this way.

"*Which* room was I born in?"

"Oh, don't be silly, do try and remember, do stop asking the same questions, haven't I *told* you . . ."

Wetherby was dumping fresh coal on to the fire, in great chunks, darkening it. He felt the warmth go off his face, a sudden shadow. Wetherby held the starched white apron flat against her body, with her left hand, out of the way of the fire. The door swung in and out again, water glasses chinked on a loaded tray. One of the bells rang. He looked up at the little, glass-fronted box. There were rows of numbers, and rows of little scarlet flaps. When somebody rang their bell, the flap dropped down and up, down and up, down and up, under the number of their room. Six, he thought, let it be six. He closed his eyes, and opened them again. But it was not six, it was nine. Nobody ever rang from six, when he was here.

"Number Six, next to the old nursery, down the corridor from Reece."

But Reece never rang her bell, either.

"Never wants anything," Aunt Spencer had said. Yet Wetherby still hated her, still grumbled, just out of earshot of the Matron, about how much trouble she was given, by Reece.

He tipped the mug of cooling milk up to his face and allowed a very little to slide into his mouth. He did not want to finish it, Wetherby would notice. "Upstairs with *you*, then, that's one thing out of the way, get along."

Wetherby had always been here, in the Cedars Lawn Nursing Home, just as Reece had always been here, in Number Seven. He hated Wetherby, and he was a friend of Reece. "*Miss* Reece," his mother made him say. And worried, vaguely, from time to time, about whether it did any harm to him, going so often to see her. But she supposed not.

He thought of how terrible it would be, if he were always in Number Seven, like Miss Reece, and always looked after and fed and woken and put to sleep and washed and chided, by Wetherby

"*Nurse* Wetherby, to you . . ."

Once, he thought that the very first face he had ever seen had been that of Wetherby, it was the thing he could remember quite clearly, from the day of his birth, in Number Six.

"What did I look like?"

"A good, healthy baby," said his Aunt Spencer, holding a white china feeding cup to the light, looking for a crack.

"*Red*," Wetherby had told him, coming behind him and whispering, on the dark stairs. "Red and ugly, that's what. You squalled."

Her top teeth were very large, and yellow, with even gaps, and they stuck out below her lip, like a bow-window. He moved away quickly.

The milk was thickish, and sweet. He held it in his mouth and swirled his tongue around inside, comforted.

"We are going out until very late. It will be much nicer for you to sleep at the nursing home," his mother had said. "It will be a treat."

He had looked away and out of the window, on to the garden, where the last of the melting snow lay, grubby as the stained linen that came down to Aunt Spencer's washroom in a hand-operated lift.

He would have said, I don't want to, I want to stay here, I don't like sleeping there all night, because of Wetherby. Once, he had half-spoken.

"*Nurse* Wetherby, to you, and you are very silly about her."

"She's ugly."

"Not everybody can be beautiful."

"Her teeth are all yellow."

"That is a nasty, *personal* remark, polite little boys do not say things like that."

"She . . ."

But he could not have told. He kept his mind turned from the thought of the upstairs landings of the Cedars Lawn Nursing Home, and the attic where he must sleep, in the room next to Wetherby.

"Are you going to a ball?"

"No, dear,"

"To a dinner?"

For they were always putting on new clothes and getting into the warm car and driving off somewhere. The names of the people whose houses they visited were familiar as those of the streets and squares around which he walked, every afternoon, with the girl Shirley, who was paid to take him out, by the hour.

"Are you going to the Mayor's Banquet, then?"

"Oh, don't be *silly*, that is in the spring. It is November now."

"*Where* are you going?"

"To play bridge with Mr and Mrs Templeton. There, now."

He knew that bridge was a game played with cards,

sitting at tables, yet whenever he heard the word, there was the same picture in his mind, of the bridge over the lake in Beecher's Park, and the railway bridge, and all the other bridges he had ever seen. He saw the people, too, his mother and father, and the Templetons and the Hoylakes and the Askew-Fishers, all rushing about on the bridges, playing some kind of elegant tag, in their evening clothes.

"Why do I have to go to Aunt Spencer's? Why can't I stay at home and be sat with?"

"Because I have told you, we shall be very late and it is altogether more convenient, that is all. Now, eat up your carrots, please."

There was only a dribble of milk left at the bottom of the mug. He looked down into it and thought about his mother, in the palely floating chiffon dress. The Templetons owned the Park Royal Hotel, facing the Esplanade. It had a monkey puzzle tree, thick and dark as felt, in the garden.

"Just *playing* with that," Wetherby said venomously, and leaned over, pushing her face close down towards him, to see the thin, liquid layer in the blue mug. He smelled her starched cotton material in the warmth from the fire, and the breath coming out from behind her yellow teeth, like the thick, stale fumes of tea.

Aunt Spencer banged through the swing doors, with Night Sister behind her, calling out that Eleven had been sick over the side of the bed and down on to the floor. He heard about it, and was unmoved, it seemed to him that the whole of adult life was about these things, the sickness and temperatures and bowels and dying, of the patients in nursing home. He was not afraid. He had always come here.

"*Bed* . . ." said Aunt Spencer suddenly, but when he looked up, he felt safe, knowing her concern for him, behind the bustling about and the care of so many patients. He had been the last child born at the Cedars Lawn Home, before they "gave up maternity". In the evenings, she had nursed him, beside the fire in her private sitting-room, warding off the recognition of her own growing old.

"Bed . . ."

He got up from the hearth stool.

"*Which* room was I born in?"

"Number Six, next to the old nursery, down the corridor from Reece."

He paused at the kitchen door, satisfied. "I could go and see her."

"Who, Reece? No. Wetherby's gone to put her on the commode."

"But I could just wait and then say good night to her."

"She doesn't want visitors at this time of night."

"It's only . . ." He looked up at the clock, but his memory failed him again, he still could not work out what the hands said, unless it were very straightforward, midday or six o'clock.

His father said, "He is very *stupid* over this matter of telling the time," and stared down at him, leaning forward a little. "I hope he is not going to be stupid in many other respects."

The fire was beginning to spurt through the new coals,

now, he did not want to leave it, and the warmth and light and smells of the kitchen, for the iron-framed bed, five flights of stairs up in the dark attics. Aunt Spencer said, "I'm going up to Eleven now, I'll come and see to you as well."

She pushed open the swing door and he followed, looking at the stiff folds of her matron's cap, streaming behind her, and the black matron's shoes, and thick, black stockings, over stout legs. He felt better, now that she was to supervise his undressing and washing and the saying of prayers. He was not going to be left to Wetherby.

Outside the door of Six, he hesitated, staring at the magic number, in gold on the brown paint, feeling the importance of it.

"Don't dawdle," Aunt Spencer said, beginning to be out of breath. "We're short-staffed tonight and Twelve is dying, I haven't time to wait about for you."

He glanced down the short corridor that led to Number Seven.

"You can see Reece in the morning."

They began to climb the next, steep flight.

Nurse Wetherby, red and puffy about the face, banged the tray on the kitchen table. He looked up and then down again, quickly, stirring his spoon through the porridge.

"Nothing but a filthy, dirty mess," Wetherby said, under her breath, "things slopped everywhere."

He flushed with alarm, and looked at the table around his plate anxiously, and down the front of his Fair Isle jumper. But there was nothing, it was not him. Reece, he thought, Miss Reece.

"It's getting worse . . . slopping everything about . . . she's not fit to live." The words came in spurts, from different parts of the kitchen, as Wetherby moved about. He knew that she was not talking to him.

Outside the window, he could see the sky, leaden with the new snow to come. He took another spoonful of sugar and tipped it slowly over the porridge, watching the brown grains spill and then sink into the soft mess, melting and leaving little stains. Aunt Spencer was upstairs with Nurse O'Keefe, laying out Number Twelve. He wondered what time his mother might come for him.

"*Dawdler*, you're as bad as that Reece, messing your food about, look at you. Huggitt's waiting to clear, I suppose you know." He stiffened. It had been quite dark when she had woken him, coming into the attic. And then her thick fingers, fumbling with his pyjamas. He thought, when my mother comes, I shall tell her, or else I shall tell Aunt Spencer, and nobody will make me sleep here again. But he knew that he would say nothing, would not know the words to use. And he was afraid of Wetherby.

The door swung open. "I thought you wanted to go and see Reece," said Aunt Spencer.

Getting down from the table, he asked who had been Number Twelve. Aunt Spencer's arms were full of rubber hot water bottles, taken out, morning-cold, from the beds.

"Mr Perrott, poor old soul." She turned to Wetherby. "There's a brother-in-law, apparently," she said, "that's all. Never been here, you see, not interested. I shall have to ring. The undertaker's coming at three."

He went out of the kitchen, and slowly up the first, linoleum-covered flight of stairs. After that, the polished wood began, and the ruby-red carpet, trodden by the shoes of the nurses and the doctors and the visitors of patients in Cedars Lawn. He thought about the dead Mr Perrott, in Number Twelve. Once he had been in to see him, but nothing was said, Mr Perrott had been asleep. He had been slightly relieved. There was always the one, bad moment, when they sent him to visit some new patient in a strange room. "Go and cheer up Nine . . . Fifteen . . . Two . . . give the poor soul a bit of company, go on." And he tapped upon the brown doors and pushed them open and went inside, and did not know what terrible things he might see.

Mr Perrott had been shrivelled, his skin and hair were the same, yellowish white. His mouth had been slightly open as he breathed. Twelve was the smallest room, facing on to the side of St Martin's Church. He had waited for a moment, politely, but Mr Perrott had not woken.

In the nursing home kitchen, Aunt Spencer had cut slice after slice of bread and said, "Cancer", in passing, to his mother.

Now, Mr Perrott was dead.

He came to the door of Number Seven. Reece. She had been here when he was born — *before* he was born. There were those, like Mr Perrott, who came for a time and died and were replaced, and those, like Miss Reece, who stayed here forever. He knocked, but out of courtesy, because there would be no answer, and then opened the door.

"Rolling in money," Wetherby said, "everything it can buy. It means nothing to them, that family of hers, nothing at all." For Miss Reece had the largest and most expensive room at the front of the Cedars Lawn Nursing Home, Miss Reece's bed overlooked the garden, and some of the furniture belonged to her family — the Sheraton dressing-table at which she would never sit, and the Persian carpet and the armchairs for visitors, and the large picture over the mantelpiece. Miss Reece lay in the high bed, and her rich family paid, the sister and the two married brothers, and an elderly aunt, and once a week, on Sunday afternoons, they visited her, by turns. They arrived in chauffeured cars, wearing coats with fur collars and doing their duty, eating tea and being bored.

He walked around the screen and crossed the Persian carpet and stood beside the high bed. It took a long time for Miss Reece to move her head on the pillow, so that she ceased to gaze out of the window, and could focus upon him, instead. He waited. Reece, about whom Wetherby always complained, rich Miss Reece, with the straight grey hair and very soft skin and the tremor in head and body, hands and legs. "Parkinson's", Aunt Spencer had said once.

He saw the recognition of him, in the slight widening of her pale eyes. On the gold, quilted counterpane, her hands lay and shook. He said, "I've just had my breakfast. I stayed here the night because my mother and father went out. They went to play bridge at the Park Royal Hotel."

Once, Miss Reece had been able to nod, but now,

he realized that he could no longer tell the difference between the nod of interest, and understanding, that was meant for him, and the helpless nodding which went on all the time.

"Did you have porridge as well? I had porridge."

Like some small, individual animal, with a life of its own, the left hand of Miss Reece twitched slightly on the counterpane. The half-moons were sketched, white as chalk, on the oval nails.

"For Christmas, I'm going to have a puppy. It's going to be a spaniel. I could bring it to see you, couldn't I? You'd like that."

The shaking continued.

He had thought that Reece was old, the oldest person in the world. She had been in her bed at the Cedars Lawn Nursing Home for eleven years. But when he had asked Aunt Spencer, she had said no, no, Reece wasn't old at all, was young, was not yet fifty, and that was the tragedy. She had had, Aunt Spencer said, "no life".

Now, he waited beside the bed, as the bell from St Martin's Church began to toll the hour. Eventually, Miss Reece would speak. He knew what she would say. It was always the same. He stood, rubbing the sole of his left sandal over the surface of his right, trying to be patient, for he must not say the words for her, must not be impolite. "She isn't soft in the head," Aunt Spencer had said. "You needn't think that, just because her speech has gone. She's all there. You must show a decent respect no matter what."

Only Wetherby muttered and grumbled, day after day, clashing the breakfast trays and the lunch trays and the trays with the visitors' teas, the jugs and bowls and bedpans, only Wetherby said, out of earshot of the Matron, that Reece was not fit to live.

He watched the small, flabby mouth begin to quiver, saw the tongue fumbling about wetly between palates, trying to grasp and form the words. There was a dribble of dried egg on one side of her chin. "Messes," Wetherby said, "messes and dribbles her food like a baby. It's getting worse and worse. I know, I have to put up with it, nobody else, I can see the way she's going. Not fit to live."

He wondered why Wetherby was a nurse, and then supposed that she could do nothing else, would not fit into any other world. He had watched her, shovelling spoonful after spoonful of liquid mess into Miss Reece's helpless mouth and never giving her enough time, making noises of impatience and imitation. But once, she had gone out of the room to answer a persistent bell, leaving the cup, and then, he had fetched a stool and stood upon it to reach the bed, and, very slowly and carefully, he had begun to put the food into Miss Reece's mouth. She had managed, there had been no dribble. But it had taken a long time. He dared not say anything to Wetherby. There would be the nights when he must sleep here, upstairs in the attic.

In the end, the words came. He understood them only because they were always the same.

"Would you like a sweet?"

It might have been some language spoken by one of a race whose mouths were shaped unlike human mouths, or else the noise of some animal, slurred and uncontrolled. He thought of what it must be like, to know the right words inside your head, to hear them there, and not to be able to bring them out, thought of words going around and around, all tangled together like washing inside a machine, trapped.

He said, "Yes, I would. Thank you very much," and waited again, for the hand to creep forwards, a little, over the gold counterpane, the forefinger to twitch, pointing as best it might, in the direction of the Sheraton dressing-table.

The box was made of tin, with a pattern painted on to it, to look like the stitchings of needlepoint, roses and leaves on a black ground. Where the lid opened and beside the hinges, the paint had been thumbed away. It had always been here, in the left-hand drawer. He knew every dent and mark upon it. It contained humbugs, striped brown and cream, in cellophane paper. Never any other kind of sweet. The humbugs were brought in by the rich relatives of Miss Reece, on their Sunday afternoon visits. She was not able to eat them herself.

He unwrapped the cellophane and put a humbug inside his mouth, and then he could say nothing, only suck at the tricklings of sweet saliva, and walk about the room, touching things lightly, looking at the picture of "The Boxing Day Meet" and the Delights of Britain's Gardens Calendar. Miss Reece lay in the high bed and shook and looked out endlessly on to the dull lawn and the empty avenue. "She likes me to go and see her," he had said to Aunt Spencer. The visits were like the words she used to answer his question.

"*Which* room was I born in?"

"Number Six, next to the old nursery, down the corridor from Reece."

Unchanging, familiar, a comfort. Miss Reece. He had always known her.

"You get along downstairs, your mother's here and waiting." Wetherby banged the door, and went straight away to Reece, heaving her up the bed, down which she always slipped, little by little every hour, unable to stop herself. He watched for a moment, and remembered the feel of Wetherby's hands, and went quickly away, not looking again into the patient eyes of Miss Reece.

"Now we are going to stay with some people in Lincolnshire, for the weekend. It is nobody you know, and there will not be any children, you would find it so dull. It will be much nicer for you to spend the whole weekend at Aunt Spencer's."

He ate the crust off a piece of toast, turning it round and round in his mouth. There had been more snow. It squeaked under the soles of his Wellington boots, as they walked to the nursing home. He was carrying his own case.

Aunt Spencer's private sitting-room smelled slightly sweet. There was a great deal of furniture, there were cushions of ruched silk and hand-embroidered pictures and firescreens and samplers and tray-cloths.

"I've cleared a space for you at my desk, you can do your drawing and painting on that," she said. "It will keep you out of everybody's way."

And so he sat for a long time in the stuffy room, fiddling with a penknife and a new box of crayons, trying to draw horses, bored. He found Lincolnshire on a tray-cloth map of Britain, and wondered about his mother and father, trying to picture the house in which they were staying.

"What are the people called?"

"Now I have already told you, darling, you have never met them, they haven't been here, to this house."

"I want to know their names. I like names."

She gave him a curious look. "How funny you are! Well, they are called Pountenay. Mr and Mrs Roger Pountenay. There!"

"Do they play bridge?"

"Oh dear, *I* don't know. Yes, I expect they do."

"Why don't they have any children in their house?"

"That is not the sort of question you should *ever* ask."

He did not know whether he would have wanted to go to the house in Lincolnshire, or not. On the wall, beside Aunt Spencer's small desk, was a carved crucifix, and a picture, in soft, blurred colours, of Jesus the Lamb of God.

He began to draw horses again.

When he heard the sound of the door opening, he woke up at once, sitting up in the bed. It was quite dark. A long way downstairs, in the kitchen, Night Nurse, with the lamp and the banked-up fire and the silent row of bells above the swing door. Nobody else. The floorboards creaked on the landing outside. Wetherby. He thought, I could do anything, shout or scream or anything, and nobody would ever hear me, and I cannot run away. He waited for the turning of the knob on his attic bedroom door. Nothing. Sounds, but going a different way, along the corridor and down the stairs.

He got out of bed and put his hands out in front of him, feeling for the door.

All the way down to the basement, the night lamps burned dimly on every landing, at the head of each flight of stairs. When he looked over the banister, he saw the back of Wetherby's head, saw her turn and go out of sight, down the corridor leading to Number Seven, the room of Miss Reece. For no reason, he felt afraid.

There was an ache in his bladder, but he dared not go down to the lavatory, on the first floor, not now. He went back into the attic and groped his way to the bed and lay, squeezing himself tightly between his legs, for fear of wetting the mattress. He did not go to sleep again. Wetherby came back. He waited, and wept with relief when her footsteps went on, past his door. It was all right, it was all right, nothing was going to happen to him. He thought about Reece.

When he woke again, he was still afraid, because he had dreamed and could not remember what he had dreamed, only felt certain that something was wrong. His pyjamas were damp, and there was a cold patch in the sheet. It was dark. There was no sound on the landing, or from downstairs, The night lights were still lit. He felt awake and not awake.

The door of Number Seven was closed. At first he did nothing, he stood outside shivering and feeling the wetness of his pyjamas. Last night, he had seen Miss Reece, he had stayed with her and eaten two sweets and talked about his mother and father in Lincolnshire and how he could not draw horses. "Turn out her light," Wetherby said, "I don't want to go traipsing back up there again." But he had not done so, it had seemed too early, too unkind, leaving Miss Reece in the dark.

Every morning, after breakfast, every afternoon, and every evening, Wetherby, and somebody helping her, stripped the bedclothes off and lifted up the shaking Miss Reece and placed her on the wooden commode. But yesterday, Wetherby had had to change everything, she said to Huggitt, sheets, blankets, the lot, it went straight through, she was filthy, she didn't try, didn't care, she couldn't bother to lift her finger and press the electric bell. She was getting worse. "Filthy," Wetherby said.

He thought, now, that by seeing Miss Reece, he might find comfort for himself.

The room was in darkness. He could hear nothing, until the door closed, and then the faint hissing of the gas.

He thought that she would be dead, and he had never seen a dead person, only the coffins being carried down the stairs by the overcoated men. But Miss Reece lay, propped on the two, full pillows, and he saw that she was not dead, she was breathing deeply, her face a little flushed and pink, in the light of the lamp.

After he had opened the window, he ran, holding his breath, and in the lavatory, on the next landing, was sick. He could not imagine what he might do, could not think of the words he could use to tell them, and be believed. Miss Reece was not dead. He must go back to bed, that was all.

On Saturdays, Wetherby did the early morning teas,

and then went away, wearing a green woollen coat and hat, caught a bus to visit her married sister in the country, eleven miles away. She did not come back until very late at night. Tomorrow was Saturday. Nothing could happen to him.

As he closed his door, he heard Wetherby open hers. Downstairs, the clock struck six-thirty. At seven, the rattle of teacups would begin. He did not sleep again.

"Something's wrong with Reece," Aunt Spencer said. He looked up quickly, from the moist centre of his boiled egg, and saw that Wetherby had come into the kitchen and was watching him, her eyes narrowed and angry, beneath the fleshy lids. He thought, she is dead after all, she is dead and it is my fault because I said nothing. Wetherby has killed her with the gas from the fire. He thought that he had done the right thing, because his father had taught him about gas, and about fires too, and fainting and deep cuts; he said, a boy should not flinch, he should learn to be prepared for any kind of accident from an early age.

"I took her tea up," Wetherby said. "She was right enough then." Her eyes were still on his face.

"Her breathing's bad." Aunt Spencer opened the enormous bottle of Dettol and began to pour.

So she was not dead, it was all right. He thought about how he could avoid having to sleep tonight in the attic room, how he might pretend to be ill, so that Aunt Spencer would let him stay on the couch in her own room. Tomorrow, his father and mother would come back from Lincolnshire, nothing would happen, nobody should know.

Aunt Spencer put a mug of hot milk down on the desk. He was trying again to draw horses. Wetherby had gone out, he had seen the movement of her green coat, past the window, and turned his head away. She knows, he thought, she watches me and knows.

"Your *bed* . . ." said Aunt Spencer.

He was silent, remembering the wet patch of mattress.

"You needn't look like that, I shan't tell your mother."

"Oh."

When she reached the door, he said, "I want to go and see Miss Reece."

"Not now you can't, Doctor Mackay's coming to her any minute."

"What's the matter?"

"Nothing much, bit of a cold, I shouldn't wonder." She went out. He remembered her saying. "Her breathing's bad," to Wetherby, and he thought of the gas and the window he had opened, on to Miss Reece's head and chest. Outside, there was more snow. He could tell nobody, there was nothing he could say. He wondered how much of it had been his dream.

"If you wrap yourself up sensibly, you can go out and play," Aunt Spencer said.

He was rolling the head of a snowman round and round the front lawn, enlarging it, when the navy-blue car of Doctor Mackay drew up, outside the nursing home. He thought, now it is all right, now Miss Reece will not die.

The snow had soaked through to his hands, matting the red woollen gloves, and making his flesh burn with cold, as though the fingers had been trapped in a door. He went on with the rolling of the snowman. A little while before lunch, Doctor Mackay came down the steps and got into his navy-blue car and drove carefully away.

In the kitchen, that afternoon, Huggitt and Nurse O'Keefe played Beggar My Neighbour with him for over an hour, banking up the fire with logs and great chunks of coal. He won four times.

"Have a cherry cough drop," said Huggitt, sorting her cards, and the smell of them came up, sweet and sharp, into his nostrils. It was snowing again, beyond the window. He thought, this is the best place to be. And perhaps Wetherby's bus will not be able to get back.

At half-past four, Aunt Spencer and O'Keefe went up with the tea trays, and at twenty minutes to five, O'Keefe came down again to the kitchen.

"Reece is dead."

He had forgotten to pretend that he was ill, and now it was too late for that. He sat on the hearth stool, drinking the hot milk.

"There's a chamber pot under your bed this time," Aunt Spencer said. He looked away from her, and tried not to think about the dead body of Miss Reece, still for ever, in the high bed. The implications of there being someone else in Number Seven, of the words "Down the corridor from Reece" ceasing to mean what they had always meant, were too much for him.

"I've telephoned to that sister of hers. Not that they care. They'll be glad to save the money, I daresay . . . mean as they're rich . . . poor soul." But there seemed to be no alarm, no surprise among them.

At ten past seven, the kitchen door opened and there was Wetherby, shaking the snow from off the shoulders of her bottle-green coat.

"Reece is dead," said O'Keefe at once.

He looked down into his milk. Wetherby went out into the hallway, in search of Aunt Spencer. Because of the bad weather, she had been shopping, just into the town, she had not tried to go as far as her married sister's.

The fire exploded and spat little slivers of coal out at him, like shell-shot. The flames were blue-green.

"Pneumonia," he heard Aunt Spencer say, swinging the kitchen door. "And Mackay's talking nonsense about the Coroner."

He felt Wetherby come across the room towards him.

"I'll take this one upstairs," she said, "and that'll be one job out of the way."

He saw her feet, misshapen and bumpy with corns, inside the black nurse's shoes. Beyond them, Aunt Spencer shook a thermometer.

"Yes," she said, "and there's a chamber pot for him, under the bed."

He followed Nurse Wetherby out of the kitchen, and up the first flight of linoleum-covered stairs.

Cockles and Mussels

Both the lounge and dining-room of the Delacourt Guest House commanded a view of the sea.

"There is nothing at all gloomy *here*, nobody has to suffer some dark, poky bedroom with outlook on to a wall," said Mrs Muriel Hennessy, the proprietress. Though she did not count the cook, Mrs Rourke.

There had been, until five years ago, a Mr Hennessy, dealer in fine wines and spirits. In the early days of their marriage, they had gone around the Châteaux of France together every spring, tasting, buying. But Mr Hennessy had begun to drink, two, and later three, bottles of sherry a day, the relationship had soured, his wife had put money aside, secretly, in a building society account.

After his death, she had waited six, decent months before leaving their bungalow in the home counties and travelling to the sea, to make her fresh start with the Delacourt Guest House.

"It has always been a little, private longing of mine," she had told her friends, giving a small sherry party to say goodbye, "to be of some service to others, give a few, retired people a very comfortable and happy home." Though, in fairness she was forced to admit to prospective clients that her charges were somewhat higher for the larger, front bedrooms.

A year ago, Miss Avis Parson had come into money from a deceased aunt, and then she had been able to take one of these, to move from a pink room overlooking the garden, into a blue room, overlooking the sea.

Mrs Hennessy was fond of saying laughingly that Miss Parson had "served her time", she deserved to come into her inheritance. For she did not like to think of any of her residents pinching and scraping, anxious about where the next month's rent was coming from.

It was not the quietness, not the gentle slope of the Guest House garden, down towards the promenade, not the different moods of the sea, for which Miss Parson was grateful. They pleased her well enough, but nothing happened, it was all a little dull.

"I am sixty-nine," she said, brushing her white hair, which was as long as it had ever been when she was a young girl, "I am not like Old Mr Brotherton, who is fit only to doze and dream and remember little incidents of his naval past. I have my eyes open to modern life and what goes on about me." For, from the side window of the blue bedroom, she could see towards the Lower Bay, and it was to the Lower Bay that the day trippers came. Mrs Muriel Hennessy, and, indeed, all the property owners and shopkeepers and residents of the upper town, held day trippers in the lowest possible esteem. "They are not *real* visitors," she would say, bringing the tea trolley with their late, hot drinks around the lounge, "they come in charabancs and throw away their litter, they do nothing for the image of the town."

And, along the foreshore and up and down the narrow streets of the Lower Bay were all the most common attractions, the souvenir gift shops full of rose-painted pottery and highly varnished shells, the ice cream and fish and chip parlours with tall stools set against eau de nil marble counters, the rifle ranges and the five shilling photographers and the sellers of novelty balloons.

At the far end of the foreshore was the Fun Fair, and, opposite the Fun Fair, beside the lifeboat house, the shell-fish booths, where cockles and mussels and winkles and shrimps were shovelled into little paper cones and sprinkled with malt vinegar.

"Everything is so vulgar on the Lower Bay," said Mrs Hennessy, "everything is so cheap and nasty, it smells so, I wonder anyone at all can bear it."

But, in her heart, Miss Avis Parson felt that life as it should be lived was lived along the foreshore of the Lower Bay. At night, she drew the curtains of her side window and sat, watching the flickering lights of the amusement arcade and the Fun Fair, saw the big wheel turn round in an arc of gold and mauve and the water chute cascade electric blue. If she opened her window, and the breeze was in the right direction, she could hear the shrieks and cries of girls as their skirts went about their heads on the swing-boats, the crack and pop of bullets on the rifle range. The hours between ten and midnight, when everything was abruptly doused and darkened, filled Miss Parson with excitement and little, sudden spurts of longing. I have lived too sheltered a life, she thought, I have never known enough about the truth of things, about what really goes on. For she had been companion to her father in his Rectory — Miss Parson the Parson's daughter, said the village children, though she did not mind — and later, to her unmarried brother in Wales, the years in which she had meant to do this and that had slipped too quickly by.

That summer, when she moved into her more expensive, blue front room at the Delacourt Guest House, the weather was almost always good, the days long and hot and the beaches bright and noisy with day trippers.

Mrs Hennessy turned away importunate families, evening after evening, at the door. "I am not a hotel for passing visitors, I am entirely devoted to the care of the elderly, of my permanent residents," she told them, smoothing down the skirts of her pastel linen dresses, watching them go off in their laden cars, hot and tired and disappointed down the drive.

In the afternoons, tea was served on the terrace and the deckchairs were occupied by old Mr Brotherton and Mrs de Vere and the Misses Phoebe and Ethel Haynes, sleeping under striped umbrellas to shade them from the glare of the sun.

Miss Parson took little solitary walks up Cliff Terrace, behind the Guest House, and the desire to venture along into the streets and shops and arcades of the Lower Bay became an obsession with her. Though she would have said nothing about it, and she was not, in any case, anxious to chat a great deal with any of her fellow guests, she saw herself as both younger than they were and somehow less permanent, for was she not entirely free, might she not suddenly choose to move on? She had money, she had her health, one day she might buy a flat in some quiet place abroad, might go on a cruise or pay an extended visit to her old school friend in Edinburgh. She reviewed her situation daily. And, meanwhile, she longed to mingle with the crowds who came in charabancs and private cars, to unmask the noisy secrets of the ghost train and eat shrimps and winkles with her fingers, sitting beside the sea.

It was only her sudden discovery of the drinking habits of Mrs Rourke which, for a short while, diverted her attention.

When the lights of the Fun Fair were switched out, Miss Parson left her chair by the window, after drawing the curtains again, and prepared herself for bed. As long as there had been something to watch and listen to, the attraction of roundabout music and the lights flickering in the sky, she was never tired, her mind was filled with pictures of the scene, couples arm-in-arm together and the mothers of grown-up families, ridiculous in cardboard hats, middle-aged romances brought to a point of decision among the dodgems. But later, in the abrupt darkness, she remembered that she was sixty-nine years old and knew nothing, was ready to climb a little stiffly into her divan bed. But before doing so, she went quietly along the corridor to the bathroom, and it was just outside the bathroom that Miss Parson first found the cook, Mrs Rourke, her eyes curiously glazed, unable to focus on Miss Parson's face, and her hand clutching at the bare wall. Mrs Rourke had been cook for seven months, at the Delacourt Guest House.

The following day, old Mr Brotherton complained again, loudly, about the quality of the mashed potato. "There are lumps," he said querulously, paddling them about in the serving dish with a spoon, "there are more lumps at every meal, every day there are more."

Rita, the daytime waitress, shot him an evil look, but in the kitchen she exaggerated the nature and number of the complaints to Mrs Hennessy.

"You needn't think the staff have never noticed," she added, balancing four vegetable dishes along her outstretched arm, "it isn't as if any of us are exactly satisfied."

Mrs Hennessy lifted a fork out of the remaining potatoes, and peered into them. She could not see any lump, and had she not had trouble and worry enough over cooks, in years past? Was this not always the season for groundless complaints? The heat was proving too much for them. She decided to say nothing.

Some nights later, Miss Parson heard the uncertain footsteps of the cook fumbling along her corridor, the slight brushing of her guiding hand, along the wall. When she opened the door, a few moments later, the faint, sour smell of Mrs Rourke's whisky hung about on the air.

In her narrow back bedroom, at the far end of the landing, Mrs Ruby Rourke lay with her coat still on, feet propped up on her pillow, and looked down at her own ankles. A fine pair of legs, for a woman your age, she thought, the finest pair of legs for miles. And her eyes filled with sudden tears of pride, that years of standing beside sinks and ovens had not thickened the muscles or spread the veins. Only her feet were bad now, the bunions sticking out like red noses on their side, under the fine stockings.

A year ago, she had been cooking for thirty-five

secretarials in a London hostel, and when they had passed her by on the stairs, going out to dinners and parties with a stream of young men, she had looked at their legs and not had any cause to envy them, had seen over-fleshed knees and thick calves, lack of any shapeliness or finesse. And they've other lessons to learn, she had thought, looking at herself in the wardrobe mirror, it takes a woman in her fifties to know how to enjoy herself. *I* wouldn't be in their shoes, wouldn't be eighteen or twenty again, thank you very much.

But in the nights she had woken and heard them clattering up the stairs, laughing inconsiderately, and had not been able to get to sleep again for hours, had been obliged to get up and search about in her wardrobe for a bottle of gin. In the mornings, the skin around her eyes looked puffed and swollen.

When she had been asked to leave the hostel, there had not been another job in London, in the end she had had to travel up here and apply to the Delacourt Guest House.

"Oh, I like old people, I like to see they get nourishing meals," she had told Mrs Hennessy, crossing her legs to reveal their elegant shape, under the short black skirt. "I couldn't get along with those young girls, oh, no, couldn't take to their noisy, selfish little ways. It was something like living in a zoo, Mrs Hennessy, and half the food picked and poked at in a *very* dissatisfied way."

"I daresay they were dieting, Mrs Rourke, that is what young girls all do, nowadays." Mrs Hennessy was looking at the careful make-up and wondering what age the woman might really be, and if there were not something a little unsuitable about vanity, in an institutional cook.

"I am fifty," said Mrs Rourke, who was fifty-seven, "and I am thankful that I have never had to diet, my figure is all that it should be."

Mrs Hennessy had inclined her head and begun to wonder about the lack of any recent references. But in the end the problem was solved for her, by the absence of any other applicant.

On the last Friday in July the temperature reached 84 degrees and the season for day trippers was at its height.

Sitting in the garden of the Delacourt Guest House, Miss Parson felt restless, felt the summer again passing her by, and was irritated with those around her, by the talk of the Misses Haynes, who were spiritualists, and the snores of old Mr Brotherton. I have no place here, she thought, it is a house for old and dying people and I shall begin to grow like them, the trivialities of everyday life here will assume a greater and greater importance, the times of meals will be all I have to look forward to. And it will be my own fault.

For she had been both startled and aroused by her discovery that Mrs Rourke came home the worse for drink. *She* has some kind of experience and pleasure, Miss Parson thought, some merrymaking and delight in life, she is a woman unafraid of the world, she has the courage of her convictions and laughs in the face of propriety. For the drunkenness of the cook seemed to her entirely romantic, it had no weak or pathetic aspect.

The hard, straight sunlight lay across the Victorian

house, and the terrace and garden, it was too hot, now, for any of the residents except Miss Parson herself, and old Mr Brotherton, snoring under a panama hat. From the beaches came the high, sharp cries of children, the sea glittered in ridges for miles out.

I have no courage, I am too concerned about the opinions of others, too afraid of their displeasure. I am anxious to walk down on to the Lower Bay and see the sights, observe the people, anxious to eat cockles and mussels and go along into the Fun Fair, and is that not a very slight, harmless ambition? Yet I have sat here for week after week and only ventured out into the respectable, upper part of the town, only walked the streets and bought from the shops approved of by women like Mrs Hennessy. It is a very poor thing. I do not deserve to have any excitement out of life, any new experiences, I am made of flimsier stuff than a cook!

In her agitation, Miss Parson got up quickly from the striped deckchair and began to walk round and round the garden, rubbing her fingers about in the palms of her hands, wanting to make a decision.

On the hot, Saturday evening, Miss Parson ate very little supper, and did not go into the lounge afterwards, to take coffee.

"I have some business in the town — a friend to see," she said hastily, in reply to the inquisitive expression of Mrs Hennessy, for none of the guests ever went far, in the evenings. But then, she was annoyed with herself, for she paid good money to live here, she was her own mistress, why was it at all necessary to explain her doings in that flustered way?

"On Saturday night, Miss Parson? Oh, are you quite sure that you are wise? The town is so full of rowdy strangers, I am a little concerned as to whether you will be quite safe."

Miss Parson would have said, and that is why I am all the more eager to go, but little Mrs Pardue, with the pink bald patch showing through her grey hair, said, "Rowdy people do not come up to *this* end of the town, I am thankful to say," and in the subsequent murmur of relief and agreement, Miss Parson slipped out.

She felt not merely excited but guilty. The Lower Bay was, in a sense, quite forbidden territory, in the tacit agreement of the residents of the Delacourt, and she could only guess at what they might say of her visit, were they to find out. One or two of them did not entirely like her. "There is just *something* about Miss Parson," Miss Phoebe Haynes had said, "she is not really altogether one of us."

On leaving Cliff Terrace, Miss Parson made a detour, up to the top of the hill and around the avenue, for someone might be watching her, unseen, from a bedroom window, and then a report would be made at once to the lounge, and to Mrs Hennessy. The ghost of Miss Parson's father warned her, as she altered course and made for the Harbour road, that she was acting a lie. The road dipped and the Guest House was out of sight. And I do not care, Miss Parson said, gripping her pouched black handbag, I have done nothing with my freedom, nothing at all, it is quite time I grasped at my opportunities and enjoyed some small, innocent adventure.

She wore well-fitting leather shoes, and a lightweight coat, in case the evening should turn chilly, for she did not intend to return early to the Delacourt Guest House.

From her back bedroom window, Mrs Rourke saw Miss Parson set out up Cliff Terrace, and then, glancing up again from powdering carefully around her eyes, saw her turn, and go off towards the Lower Bay.

"Well!" she said to her own image in the mirror, and was taken once again by the elegance of her own figure, the shapeliness of leg and ankle. She had always insisted, at every place of employment, upon Saturday as one of her regular nights off, everything happened on a Saturday, you never knew your luck.

For a long time Miss Parson simply walked slowly along the pavements, looking at people's faces. These are the old and the modern young, mingling together, she thought, these are the day trippers, this is life. Middle-aged men in shirts, open over sun-reddened chests, wore pressed-paper hats in imitation of cowboys or undertakers or policemen, and Miss Parson stared into their eyes, anxious to learn the secrets of enjoyment. It was very crowded, very warm in among the booths and cafés, the night air flashed with multi-coloured lights, and along the pier they bobbed, orange and green and red, reflected in the dark sea.

I am very happy, I am watching the world go by, discovering things I never knew, Miss Parson told herself, sitting down on a foreshore bench while she emptied sand out of her shoes, there is nothing to be ashamed of or snobbish about it, that I can see. Loudspeakers sent the metallic beat of popular music out across the street.

Somewhere, far down beyond the green railings and the piled-up deckchairs, the long, pale shelf of sand, the edge of the sea, creaming and stirring a little in the darkness. I would like to walk there, too, thought Miss Parson, it is many years since I have been on a beach at night. Though as children they had spent their holidays at Bexhill, and she had walked the dog Beaver out, after dark, smelling the salt and the green smell of seaweed and imagining her own future, filled with rich, nameless excitements.

A car began to hoot on the roadway, nosing into the back of jaywalkers. Miss Parson got up and went across to the Seagull Milk Bar, to perch uncertainly on a high stool with tubular steel legs and drink a cup of expensive tea. All around her, everyone moved, laughed and chatted across the tables, over plates of waffles and haddock, peas and chips, and every movement reflected brightly in the mirrors above the counter, so that Miss Parson, watching, felt uncertain of which was real and which the image. Under a table, a small child in green bathing trunks dribbled lemonade gently on to its bare legs from the end of a straw.

"There you go, my duck," a man said, helping her down from the precarious stool, and she noticed the reddish hairs, matted all the way up his arms.

But it was going through the glittering golden archway of the Fun Fair, and standing just a little way inside, which brought home to her where she had come, alone on a Saturday evening, how many unwritten rules of proper conduct she had disobeyed. For a moment, she held her breath and was doubtful, would have gone quickly away, the noise and the clamour of people and machines and lights around her was more than she felt able to take. The smell of the place came out towards her. But then, she went ahead, fumbling in her purse for money, and joined the queue leading to the switchback railway.

On the fourth, reckless plunge over the crest of the metal track and down, down, slicing into the darkness, Miss Parson opened her eyes and saw that the woman next to her was clutching on to her sleeve, eyes huge in her melon-shaped face.

"Oh!" she said, "Oh!" and the hand gripped tighter, though no sound coming out of the woman's mouth could be heard above the noise, there was only the purse of her lips, purple-looking under the artificial lights. She is laughing, Miss Parson realized suddenly, there is nothing wrong with her whatsoever, she is simply laughing, and she felt friendly, warmed by the careless grasping of the stranger's hand, the gesture of conviviality on the switchback.

As they climbed and plunged again, Miss Parson thought of old Mr Brotherton, and of Mrs Hennessy, stout and managerial in a linen dress, and began to laugh, to feel superior to all of them, as one who has outwitted everyone else in the battle of life, discovered some amazing secret.

Returning to the ground again, she was obliged to lean for some moments against the ticket booth, unable quite to recover her breath. Overhead, the big wheel spun in a flashing circle, as if gathering speed to take off like a top into the sky.

The cockles were hard to eat, she was uncertain which way to prise them out of their hard, little shells, and in her mouth they tasted as they smelled, strong as brine and heavily vinegared. But there was something rich and coarse and satisfying about eating such things, and about queueing up to buy more, to hover in her choice between the brown-pink whiskered shrimps and mussels, rubber-smooth and yet curiously gritty in the mouth.

The foreshore was now more crowded than ever, the voices more raucous, shrieking and cat-calling and squabbling, now and then. Miss Parson got up from her bench when the man next to her began to slip sideways heavily and to snore like old Mr Brotherton, huge hands upturned and loose on his trousers. But, after all, it is only another human being, she told herself, only another aspect of life, and she felt herself expanding and blossoming with new insights and knowledge, open to a stream of experience.

A trickle of juice was left in the paper cone after she had eaten the last mussel, so that, in screwing it up, she stained her coat sleeve. The smell was blotted at once into the cloth, and came up sharply into her nostrils. It would stay there, now, certain proof, in all the months to come, of her evening in the Lower Bay, her new-found courage.

A gang of men and girls came stepping out in a row, arms linked, breasting the whole width of the road, and singing, and for a second Miss Parson was caught up among them, she could see the white teeth and peacock-painted eyes of the girls, smell the men's sweat, and then they parted and went on like the tide, leaving her behind.

In the orange-painted Bingo Booth, open out on to the street, a game finished and, looking up from her unsuccessful card, the cook, Mrs Rourke, saw Miss Avis Parson. Earlier, she had found one or two people to talk to, someone had bought her a drink, but it had come to nothing, the bar had emptied and filled up again and she was left to apply fresh lipstick and do something herself about the empty glass.

"Well, now!" she said, therefore, touching Miss Parson lightly on the arm, for familiar company was suddenly better than none, better than the old routine of trying to strike up a new acquaintance. "Well, here's a thing!"

Though a thought crossed her mind, to wonder if the old girl might not be a bit unwell, a bit wandering all of a sudden, standing down here and smelling of shell-fish and vinegar on a July Saturday night. She had always had a peculiar fear of madness.

"It has all been a splendid treat, Mrs Rourke, this is a whole new world to me. I have been telling myself for so long, promising myself, you know, that I would be as bold as could be and venture down among the holidaymakers, and now here I am! But I am really just a little bit tired, I do confess to you, my feet are feeling rather swollen."

It did not surprise her, for nothing was surprising now, when Mrs Rourke, too, took hold of her arm.

"It's the sand," she said, confidentially, nodding into

Miss Parson's face, "the sand gets into them, plays them up. You can't tell me."

"Yes? Well then, that is very likely the case and perhaps I have had enough for one day, perhaps I should be getting home . . ."

Miss Parson thought that the cook might be older than she looked, though she admired her care for her own appearance, the brightness of rouge and lipstick and the height of her heels. They were walking uphill now, between the last of the gift shops, and away from the sea, and Miss Parson saw that everyone, here, was arm-in-arm with everyone else, it must be the way of things, the air was close with bonhomie.

"My treat, dear," said Mrs Rourke, making her way firmly between backs and elbows to the lounge bar. "What's it to be?"

But, sitting at the little, low table and surreptitiously easing a shoe from off one of her feet, Miss Parson felt depressed, thought perhaps it is all a little aimless, all too trivial to count as life, perhaps I have been wrong to come riding on switchbacks and eating strange food and drinking sweet sherry in the Lower Bay.

Mrs Rourke was telling her some story, her eyes protruberant in a flushed face, and Miss Parson thought of the nights when she had found her leaning unsteadily against the Guest House wall, wondered in a moment of panic where it would all end.

Mrs Rourke had forgotten exactly who she was with, was launched, now, into the full tale of her bad treatment at the hands of her previous employers, the London secretarial school.

"Take no nonsense, good cooks are in short supply, my hubbie would have said." She wiped lipstick carefully off her glass with the corner of a handkerchief. "He was a chauffeur," she told the dazed Miss Parson. "There wasn't anything you could tell Rourke about the tricks of employers."

"I think I really should like to be getting back now," said Miss Avis Parson. But when she stood, the lounge tipped and spun round, there was a curious, high-pitched echo inside her head.

In the Delacourt Guest House, Mrs Hennessy switched off the parchment-shaded lamps in the lounge, and closed the top windows, wondering if she had been wise to let Miss Parson have a key.

The whole street seemed to be singing, now, everyone came pouring out on to the pavements as the stalls and cafés began to close, and the smell of beer and human bodies mingled with the faint ozone of the sea.

"Steady she goes," said Mrs Rourke, stepping off the kerb and on to it again sharply. "Take it gently."

"Oh, the nice fresh air, the nice, *nice*, fresh air."

Can't hold a drink, thought Mrs Rourke with disgust, doesn't know the first thing about it. Aloud she said, "We're two merry lonely old ladies," as they came up the Harbour road, leaving the trippers behind them, facing the stairs, "two lonely old souls."

There is something wrong, thought Miss Parson, something very wrong indeed, I do not wish to be here, led along the street by a drunken cook, and called an old woman and lonely, there is nothing at all like that about me, and she can know nothing. I would prefer to forget this incident. But, climbing Cliff Terrace, her legs felt weak under her and she was obliged to hold on to Mrs Rourke's arm again for a little support.

"It's a bit of a hole, Miss Parson, a bit of a one-eyed hole. I'm used to a good deal better than this, I deserve it, you know, this is not the sort of carry-on I'm accustomed to."

I do not trust you, Miss Parson thought, I have learned a very great deal tonight, about the ways of the world, and I do not feel able to trust you, you will not get away with anything with me. But she could not altogether follow what the other woman was saying.

"Come along, old girl."

But Miss Parson had stopped and bent over to examine her shoes. Behind them, the lights of the Fun Fair were gutted, the whole of the bay was given over once more to the incoming sea.

At four, Miss Parson woke in severe abdominal pain, so that, after staggering to the bathroom and back again, she collapsed at the side of her bed and was forced to crawl up, hand-over-hand, and ring the service bell.

Towards morning, the doctor was called, for the pain and sickness had worsened, she became delirious and then semi-conscious.

At breakfast in the dining-room there was an air of alarm and expectancy, questions were asked and speculations aroused, and old Mr Brotherton refused to eat more than a triangle of toast. "It is the cook," he muttered, leaning forward and speaking up so that he should be heard quite clearly at all the tables, "the food is bad, it is not surprising that Miss Parson has been taken ill. Something should be said to the cook, I have said so before, I hope you will all bear me out."

So that, throughout the next few days, when Miss Parson's condition worsened and, in the end, she was taken to the hospital, the cry grew louder of "the cook, the cook" as a crowd might mutter, "Guilty! Guilty! Off with her head!" and Mrs Hennessy, who had discovered the gin and whisky bottles in Mrs Rourke's wardrobe, felt that more than goodwill was now at stake, something public would have to be done.

"It is acute food poisoning," she told Mrs Rourke, sitting at the desk in her tidy office, "the doctor is extremely worried, Miss Parson is quite dangerously sick."

Nor was she pleased when the lies came out so glibly, the long, garbled tale about Miss Parsons's eating cockles and mussels and drinking alcohol in the Lower Bay. For surely they were lies, she thought, when the cook had been formally dismissed, surely the aloof, prim little Miss Parson would never have been so foolish? Though Mrs Hennessy recalled that there had so often been a strange look on her face, a furtive, secretive expression, and perhaps she had been growing a little senile, perhaps there was a hardening of the arteries and she had begun to act in that way common among the old, as though a new, alien personality had been suddenly assumed.

Well then, it will not do for her to come back *here*, for this is only a Guest House, not a nursing or a geriatric home, I am neither trained nor equipped nor willing to cater for the senile and unreliable, the responsibility would be altogether too great. She thought that there were no relatives of Miss Parson, but somewhere, an old school friend — in Edinburgh? Or perhaps, simply, the doctor could fill out a form and the whole thing be done locally, some suitable home would be quickly found.

In the event, that was not necessary, Miss Avis Parson died in her bed at the General Hospital of a heart attack, following the ravages of food poisoning. The doctor, bringing the news to Mrs Hennessy, warned against any future use of shellfish, cockles or mussles, shrimps or crab, in the cooking at the Delacourt Guest House.

"Old people," he said, almost apologetically, standing on the doorstep beside his car, "nothing indigestible, nothing, really, in the seafood line, Mrs Hennessy, take my advice upon it."

It was only out of respect for the memory of the recently deceased Miss Parson that she did not speak of her own, long-existing ban on all crustacea from the menus of the Delacourt.

On the train, Mrs Rourke lifted her coat up on to the rack, tidied up her face in the tiny, rectangular mirror and then walked along to the buffet car for a drink. She had found, only the day after her dismissal from the Guest House, an appointment as cook to a boys' approved school in rural Norfolk. They had not asked for an interview or anything more than verbal references simply because they were, they said, desperate, they would take her on a month's probation.

Like one of the bloody inmates, Mrs Rourke thought bitterly, imagining the remoteness of the countryside, the absence of any Gaiety and Life, like a bloody prisoner myself. But then she rebuked herself, for she did not like to swear, it was a sign of weakness, a loosening of her grip. Instead, she looked down into her glass for a moment, and then drank, quickly, to the memory of the seaside, and of Miss Avis Parson.

Somerville

Even the sight of the envelope terrified him. For he did not receive letters now — only a few household bills and their receipts, a random circular. This was what he had planned, that he should retire here and nobody should disturb him, that he should be forgotten. There would be no letters. The envelope terrified him.

So that, for comfort, he went to his desk and found that other letter and sat with it on the terrace in the early morning sun, weighing it in his hand, and he despaired again.

He had no need to read it, knowing the words by heart, but he read it and the shape of the letters upon the page helped him, the familiarity of the emotions they aroused. The sun was already hot upon his face, though it was not yet ten o'clock. These days, it was always hot.

"Somerville", it began, the twenty-seven-year-old letter, "Somerville", as though they had reverted to the formality of first acquaintance, as though this were no time for the frivolity of Christian names. "Somerville", and he looked up, and into the sun, remembering how it had been, how he had sat at his desk in Whitehall and seen his own name upon the scuffed page and already known, for over two months, that Barton was dead. "Somerville" . . . The sight of the envelope had terrified him. Beyond the tall windows St James's Park, and a steel-blue sky, the January sun glinting on the lake and the stiff backs of ducks, down between bare trees. "Somerville" . . .

Now, he took the letter out of the envelope again and unfolded it, and still it seemed that nothing so appalling could ever come to him again, that he would never be so troubled by the sight of handwriting upon a sheet of paper.

Somerville,

I can't write much now. I can't think. My fingers are almost gone — I mean, frozen. They swell up and stiffen. Though holding a mug is the worst — hot tea — they warm up and you can't stand it, the skin cracks open. You don't care about anything here, except the bloody cold, and keeping yourself moving, on your feet, keeping on. I think about you when I can. Sorry.

Listen, yesterday we dug Lewis Higton out. I mean dead, he was frozen, he'd gone in up to the chest and you don't last long in this, if you go down — ten, fifteen minutes? I don't know. I suppose he fell. You can't notice anything in this, you can't think of anything except yourself. We went back for him. But we dug him out and he was dead. I thought you'd want to know. Though there are enough of us dead aren't there, for Christ's sake, how many of us are left? You're left, I suppose. I don't know. We don't get news.

I can't write, not much, I can't hold the pen, but I can tell you, I know what hell is and it isn't hot, it's cold, it's this frozen, bloody country. You want to lie down and just go off, you know, just give up. They won't let you. But maybe he did that, Lewis Higton. Maybe. I don't know. I don't know how long we'll be either, they don't tell us anything. We'll be no use when we get there. They say it's pretty bad, there isn't any food. But you can't tell, you don't care, not about anything except yourself, keeping yourself going. Yesterday one of the prisoners went mad with a can-opener and they shot him. Dunkerly shot him. He had strange eyes, walnut-coloured eyes. I can't get him out of my head. Dunkerly shot him and I remember him, I dream about him, the colour of his eyes. It's bloody silly things like that you remember. I've changed, you wouldn't know me, you won't ever know me, not after this.

I can't write, my fingers are hopeless, I can't move the others, the ones on the left hand, can't feel them at all. Only thought you'd care to know about Higton, He played the piano, didn't he? The one in your rooms. Bloody silly things like that go through your head. Higton playing your piano. We shouldn't have dug him out, should we, we should have left him there, just left him.

Jesus, this cold, Jesus.

After that, Somerville had wanted nothing to do with letters. He did not want this letter, today.

Shortly after coming here, six years ago, he had realized that he could no longer remember what Barton looked like. There had once been a photograph, a single snapshot, of the three of them, Barton and himself and Lewis Higton who died in the snow, they had stood together awkwardly, in tennis flannels and with white pullovers tied about their necks, racquets dangling from long arms, and all of their faces looked oddly similar, bony and eager, and blurred, the hair of all their heads appeared thick and pale. But the picture never served to remind him of anything. Barton had not looked like that, and in the end the photograph had been lost or burned or thrown away, and now he could not remember. There had only been the letter, coming to him like a ghost, weeks after Barton's death.

On his own sixtieth birthday, when he was already retired and settled here, the shock of imagining Barton, alive and of the same age, Barton, at the mercy of stiffening joints and weakening eyes and greying hair, had been very great. Though later he had been comforted, knowing that, after all, it was not true, that Barton was dead and therefore could not change, was now as he had always been. Only that the image of him was faded and dispersed as the flesh itself, now, within Somerville's mind. And every so often, he took out and re-read the letter.

"Somerville" . . .

All his life, he had planned to live here. He had seen it first on the day he was taken to meet his great-uncle, the famous general, they had driven past the tall gates in his father's car and he had looked through them and up the long drive between the beech trees, to the rose-brick house. The car was an early de Dion, slow upon the hills, he had hated it from the beginning, sitting in the front upon his mother's lap, and feeling as though they were on the back of some monster. But that day, climbing up slope after wooded slope of the Chilterns, into the sun, he had been soothed, began to come to terms a little with the terrible car and with the driver, his father, as he might, after many hours of cautious watching and stroking, with some wild animal. And then he had seen the gates and, through their black patterns, the drive, and the garden and terrace and rose-coloured brick, the glint of the lake and the magic shape of the chimneys. Moving very slowly past in the car had been better than walking, for there had been enough time, but none in which the sight of the place could become over-familiar, they had not gone up too close.

Though perhaps he realized none of it, until he was grown up, perhaps imagination supplied this and that detail. Certainly, he remembered nothing else about that day, nothing about the visit to the famous general. Only the fact that his father had been, for once, good-tempered, and then the slowly moving picture of the house, glimpsed through gates at the end of a drive.

Years later, he and Barton had come walking here, day after day through the whole of one summer, searching. But when the house was at last found, he would come no nearer than the gates, not wanting the place to deliver up, before he was ready to take them, any of its secrets. He had returned to Oxford, and later to London, to his mathematics, a spare, rational, ascetic man, a believer in the symmetry and clarity of life, obsessed by the beauty of the knowledge that the world contained five regular solids, no more and no less, a romantic.

So that when he was almost sixty, and he read that the house was for sale, he was unsurprised, he bought it and relinquished his public posts, the advisory positions in Whitehall, his fellowship at the university, his membership of committees. He was untroubled, too, by the fact that the house had come to him rather earlier than he might normally have expected to retire, looking upon these extra years as a gift, the margin of incalculable bounty for which one allowed, in a calculable world.

He negotiated the entire purchase through an agent and from a distance, in order that the day after his official retirement should be the first upon which he walked any further than the tall gates, walked up to and into the rose-brick house, from the long drive. He thought, I have everything that I shall ever want, for the rest of my life. Though, in his breast-pocket, there was the letter from Barton, which he knew by heart.

I have everything.

From that day he wished to receive no more letters. Few came.

Early that evening, he walked down the slope behind the house, to the lake. It had been made out of a gravel pit, more than a hundred years ago, long after the building of the house — to be filled with fish, for the entertainment of weekend sportsmen. Now, whatever fish might be there, he left alone. It was a small lake, entirely surrounded by a grassy path, and then by the beeches. In winter, through the pale trunks, the house could be seen, and in the opposite direction, a mile away, the village. But now, the leaves were dense green, layer upon layer. The water of the lake was completely still. Down here, the heat gathered, kept in by the trees, so that by the end of the day the air above the surface of the water shimmered, playing tricks with the light.

Somerville sat down and at once felt the letter again, stiff and flat inside his pocket. He had not opened it, he was still terrified by the sight of the envelope.

He thought, no, nothing more can happen, it can be nothing, nothing at all, no one shall come.

If he half-closed his eyelids, the lake seemed to expand and thin out, far away, he could see no end to it, which was what he would have liked, for there to have been some mystery on the other side.

The sun slipped down further, so that the water flamed.

He remembered, as he persistently remembered, the story, in Beowulf, of the burial of Scyld Scefing.

At Oxford, it had been Barton who made him read, he had come to his rooms sometimes, when Somerville was out, and left a book upon the desk, with a marker, on which would be a page, or a chapter reference, and what the book contained was always a surprise. At first, he had begun to read reluctantly, dutifully, for at that time he cared only for the preciseness of figures, not for the formlessness of words, spread about the page. But later, he always read on, caught by this or that image, amazed by what Barton was showing him, needing to discover the end of a story, the secret of a character. He read on, too, because he could never bear to leave anything incomplete, could not set down even a very bad novel, once begun, because the recollection of the loose end would have continued to irritate him. But Barton never gave him very bad novels.

After a time, he had understood that the form of words was as precise and complete as the form of numbers, and then he had become adventurous, begun to look in the windows of bookshops, try this and that for himself, and Barton had smiled and shaken his head, gently triumphant.

From the beginning, Beowulf had obsessed him, and for the rest of his life the image returned again and again, without warning, to his mind, of Scyld Scefing, the dead Danish king, laid in the ring-prowed ship among his own treasure, the riches of a lifetime, and sent off to some unknown destination across the water.

> Then high above his head they placed
> a golden banner and let the waves bear him
> bequeathed him to the sea.

Now, the thought of burning, or of earth burial, repelled him. It was this, the ship across water, which had meaning. And he had been stirred by the thought of honour. "A golden banner," he had said occasionally, to Barton, as his name in mathematics became celebrated, his opinion sought after. "A golden banner, be good enough to remember that, that will be the way to go!" Barton had smiled and shaken his head, not an envious man.

These days, Somerville found his mind filling suddenly with the image as he was doing some job, making coffee in the early morning, pruning forsythia, watching for the hedgehog, and he would be momentarily troubled, as he realized what it was that he was seeing, in his mind's eye, the burial ship moving slowly across water, the golden banner.

He thought, I have everything, I am altogether alone, there are no letters, no one calls, I have everything, and perhaps I will not be able to bear it, such an absence of anxiety and striving, perhaps this will make me mad.

But he was not truly alarmed.

The lake had darkened again, blood-red in the centre. He eased his legs, began to think of the walk back up the slope, of lighting the lamps and cooking the mackerel for supper, of the hedgehog's coming.

It was then that he heard the footsteps behind him in the grass. As he did so, he remembered, again, the unopened letter.

She had been to this house before, perhaps half a dozen times in all his six years, but never this way, only up the drive, to leave the box of groceries at his side door. Generally it was her father who came, a little, bossy man in an old green van. Or her brother. Occasionally, Somerville had caught sight of her in the shop, when he took his order, or else from a distance, walking down the street, or out along the Hadly road, towards the bus-stop. They were people with whom he had nothing in common, nothing to do, dull people whom he wished well and did not understand. He knew the name of the girl, Martha, and he had seen, some weeks before, that she was pregnant. He thought nothing of it, was uninterested. He was alone here, he had the house, everything he wanted. Nobody came.

She said, "This is where they catch fish."

Somerville got awkwardly to his feet, a little stiff and damp from the grass, and terrified of her, bewildered as to why she might have come. He could think of nothing to say.

The sun had gone altogether now, there was simply the declining evening, still warm, smelling of leaves.

"Do you?"

"I?"

"Catch the fish. Is that what you do here, all the time?"

"No." He hesitated. "No."

She laughed. "You're about the only one that doesn't, then, aren't you?"

"No one comes here, there is no one to catch the fish."

Her face shone with a rather benign amusement. Somerville felt uncomfortable, at a loss.

"That's all you know, then!"

He lifted his hands up and down inside the pockets of his jacket, wanting her to go away, unwilling to talk.

"You'd be surprised who comes up here. They *all* come. Fancy you not knowing!"

"Who comes?"

"Oh, people, this one and that one. Boys from down the village."

"To fish?"

"Why not?"

He said, "No," and shook his head, "I see no one."

"Well, you don't suppose they come dancing about your lawn, do you, they don't make a great deal of noise. It's like a game, sort of, like poaching. Except they all think you know, really. Everybody thinks that."

"I know nothing of any of it."

"Oh, I suppose you'll go and stop them now, then." Her mouth was sulky. "You'll get a dog."

"I dislike dogs."

"Well, something. Come down and send them off, spoil it for them."

He looked out across the lake, thinking. Then, after a moment, he said, "I do not care. I do not care who catches the fish, I am not interested in fish. It is not the fish that matter."

"Look, they wouldn't touch anything else, don't you start thinking that, they're not out to burgle you, are they? They're not like that, it's only catching fish, they're not going to come thieving."

"*Who* are they?" He turned and looked at her closely for a moment.

"People. I told you. Lads from the village. Dave, sometimes. Well, not so much now, he's got older, he's got other things to do. He used to."

"Your brother came here?"

"Yes."

"Do you come?"

"I'm not bothered about fishing, am I? Not that they are, really — well, not about the fish. That's not what they come for. It's like a game, I told you, creeping up through the trees and sitting here, knocking off some of your stuff from the lake. They sling them all back, generally. They come up at night. It's nothing. It's a lark, that's all."

"No."

"I shouldn't have bloody said anything. You'll come down and put up wire, you'll stop them, now, I know."

"No."

There was silence. He felt her staring at him, examining his hair and face and clothes, the way he stood, the shape and size of his feet. He would not have it, would not be looked at.

He said desperately, "I have no interest in them, I do not care what they do. So long as I do not have to meet them. So long as nobody comes near to me." For he was suddenly panic-stricken, imagining hordes of strangers trampling up through the woods, shouting and calling, setting up rods and lines and green umbrellas, eating picnics and then overflowing up the slope towards the house, into the house, invading him, his silence, passing the word round, importing friends. About the fish he cared nothing. He looked at the girl, Martha. She grinned. "They won't bother you. It's not you they're interested in, is it? You just said. You never saw them up till now, never heard them. Besides, it's only once in a way. They won't bother you."

When he had first come here, he had seen her playing about in the yard at the side of the shop, or walking to school, and she had been a child, then, with thick, short hair cut level to her chin and straight, heavy limbs. It did not seem to him long now, not more than months, though it was six years. But she was very young now, the flesh of her face was soft, still disguising the bone structure, though there was something new in her expression, a knowingness, and her eyes were narrower, tired at the corners. The child she was carrying seemed not to be part of her, it was simply a swelling, a weight carried as a bag might be carried, and behind it, she was herself, her bones and flesh were the same, unaffected, and when the child was gone, she would look as she had always looked. He supposed she might be seventeen.

She came forward abruptly and stood, hands in the pockets of her yellow dress, looking down at the water. She said, "I couldn't stick it." Somerville did not answer, he was thinking again of the house, and the lighted lamps, wanting his supper. It was time to put out milk for the hedgehog, to sit and wait on the terrace. The best time of the day.

"They don't stop, you know, that's what made me come out tonight. They can't seem to give it a rest. Round and round and round, as if we haven't had it all before, all said, right from the start. I don't know what they'll do after, when I've had it, there'll be nothing for them to talk about, will there, not for any of them?" She glanced up quickly. "Only you."

"Me?"

"Oh, they talk about *you.* You're like the weather, always good for a chat, you are."

He was astonished, and angry, too, for he had not thought himself of any interest. He was entirely separate, he did not want to exist in the minds and mouths of any of these people, it was as though a part of himself had been broken away and scattered about like crumbs to the birds, he felt diminished.

"Well, it's only natural, isn't it? You're different, you're not like anyone else round here. They can't make you out, they're always wanting to know what you're up to. I suppose I do, as well. I want to know."

She stirred her toe about in the grass. A slight breeze moved towards them, over the surface of the lake, Somerville felt it and was made anxious.

"Only just for the moment, it's me, and that's a lot more interesting, they've got me down there, haven't they, all the time, they see me every day, so it reminds them, and off they go again. It's all right for you. They hardly ever see you."

"No."

"I'll be glad when it's over and everything's back to normal, I will."

He was amazed by her, he thought, I know nothing. And then, I do not want to know.

"I was thinking about you today," she said, "I've thought about you a lot just lately. Funny that. I never did before, not much."

"You know nothing about me." He spoke stiffly, for that was what mattered, nobody should know.

"I wished I was you though, all the same. Up here all by yourself, doing what you like, Nobody says, don't do that, who was it, what are you going to do now, what did I always tell you, what do you think everybody's going to say? You don't have that, not any of it. I thought, that's what I'd like, to be up there all by myself, just like him. I wouldn't give tuppence for any of them then. That'd be all right."

Somerville smiled. "Yes."

"Only I couldn't. It's not the same for me."

He shook his head, for he did not know, and he felt battered, now, by her flow of talk, the questions and comments and desires, it was years since he had spoken for so long with another person.

"Don't you go mad, though? Don't you get lonely?"

But she scarcely paused for answer. "I would. That's why I'd never do anything like it, not really. I did wonder, I did think I might go off somewhere, on my own. I can't stand being with them. Only I'd go potty. If I were *you*, I'd go potty, up in that great house with nobody to talk to, nothing to do."

"Oh, there is everything to do!"

"What?" Her face was sharp as a monkey's. "What is there to do?"

Somerville moved a hand vaguely, not replying, trying to think of what he did. He thought, nothing, I do almost nothing. I read a little, things I have read before, I do the garden, walk about, I spend hour after hour trying to make the acquaintance of a hedgehog, I cook and clean and wash and dress and sleep and sit in the sun. Everything. Nothing.

"They all think you live in a pigsty. Up here. You don't even have anybody from the village to do for you. They think you must live in a right old muck-heap."

He was angry. "I am extremely fastidious. I am clean and tidy and neat, I care a great deal about those things."

"Oh yes. I can see that. Just by looking at you I can see it. It wasn't what *I* ever thought."

It was almost dark, the sky above the copse was only a little paler than the water of the lake. Moths had come out.

Somerville said, "You had better go home."

"I'm all right."

"No. You should not do this, walking about on your own in the woods at night, you should go home. Think — think of what might happen to you. You should not be here." For though his ideas were vague, about the behaviour of young girls, the dangers of this countryside, yet he remembered things, said years ago by his mother and his sister.

She laughed, and then she spoke again, the tone of her voice was changed, there was the hard edge of adult experience and irony, making him again uncomfortable.

"There's nothing much else can happen to me, is there? Not just for the moment." And she laughed again, so that the sound of it echoed around the circle formed by lake and trees and sky. Somerville turned and walked abruptly away. And then stopped, for should he not do something, see her back on to the road, take her home, make some gesture towards her welfare? She was a child, he felt somehow responsible.

When he looked back again, she had gone. Her dress and face and limbs had been pale, and now there were only the dark spaces between the beech trees, he could scarcely make out the place where she had been standing, across the grass.

He began to walk back to the house. But the pleasure was gone, he cared nothing for the thought of sitting on the warm terrace waiting for the hedgehog, for cooking the mackerel, smelling its rich smell, he felt dissatisfied, sour.

"They talk about you."

All the same, he lit the lamps and took out the fish and made the bread and milk in the blue saucer. But then he was restless, so that he sat outside for only fifteen or twenty minutes, and for the first time in weeks, the hedgehog did not come. Though perhaps it came later, something came, for in the morning the bread and milk were gone.

It was on waking, a little before seven, that he remembered again the unopened letter.

The sun was already hot. He went down into the kitchen and filled the kettle and made his coffee, and later, went to spray the greenfly from the roses.

That day, the postman did not come up the drive, there were no letters.

For two nights, the hedgehog stayed away. Somerville sat on the terrace in despair. Something had changed, a pattern was broken, with the arrival of the terrible letter. He had hidden it now, at the very back of a drawer in his desk. Unopened.

The days were still hot, all of that summer had been hot, he began to imagine how it would be in the world beyond this house, people talking on and on about the weather, the sun, the sun, you felt a new person, didn't you, when the sun shone, felt you could cope with anything really, so long as it didn't get too hot, because we had everything, didn't we in this country, provided you got your weather with it, everything.

He opened all the windows of the house and ate and read and sat and slept outside on the terrace, his shirt unbuttoned. In the early mornings, the air smelled of the Loire valley. But he was anxious. The hedgehog had been coming every night since the middle of April, and now it did not come.

In the end, he went down to the bottom of the garden, to the tree with the hollow. There was a lump, covered with bits of twig and leaf, which might have been the hedgehog, sleeping, but he dared not disturb it, for fear of frightening it permanently away. Once, he had seen it in full daylight, down in the grass by the old shed, basking on its belly in the sun. He changed the food in the blue saucer, cooked strong-smelling fish. He was fascinated by what the animal would and would not eat, by the way it snuffled across the terrace, towards the saucer with its moist pink snout.

Still it did not come. For comfort, he read the Japanese poetry book.

> In my boat that goes
> Over many salt ways
> Towards the open sea
> Faintly I hear
> the cry of the first wild goose.

At midday, the temperature went up to eighty, cracks opened in the lawn. He spent hours watering the rose Albertine, flowering like pink snow over the south wall.

* * *

The next time she came, he was sitting on the terrace, limbs loose in the chair, doing nothing at all, thinking nothing. He heard no footsteps. The lawn and the beech trees and the sky faded into one another like the blotted edges of a watercolour, green-blue. Then, the girl's pale shape at the top of the path.

Ever since Barton's death, he had been troubled by dreams of ghosts, rising out of mist and water and softly piled snow. Whenever he walked to the lake he expected to see something, the arm that held the Sword Excalibur. He was haunted by these few images, they had become part of him, like the burial ship of Scyld Scefing. Terrifying. He needed Barton to mock him.

Now, he stood up, knocking over the flimsy deckchair as he did so, furious, wanting to lift up a newspaper and flap the girl away, like some insect, to shout at her. He began to sweat, feeling himself spied out and known.

I have finished with your world, I have come here, chosen this place, I would be entirely forgotten.

"It's cooler up here, anyway."

Somerville bent and retrieved the deckchair, struggled to replace the awkward struts and they defied him, going over backwards so that the canvas billowed out.

"I like your garden."

He tipped the chair, dropped it down flat, began again.

"I like those flowers. What are they? Those blue ones?"

"Larkspur."

"I like those."

A willow warbler started singing from the blackthorn, at the bottom of the lawn.

"It's all of a piece, this garden, you know? There's hundreds of different things, plants and bushes and that, and they all look just anyhow, but really they're not, are they, not when you look? It wasn't like this before you came. You should have seen it in the old days."

He was still standing, hovering, as a man in a room waiting for a woman, who has just entered, to sit down. Except that he wanted her to go away.

"We used to come up here, after school, a whole lot of us did. It was empty for quite a bit, wasn't it? Well, all of one summer, anyway. It was up to your middle, then, in grass and stuff. That's years ago, though."

"No. Six years."

"Well . . .!"

He looked at her. When she was born, I was a middle-aged man, Barton was long dead. The best things were already over.

"I like it up here."

Somerville sat down heavily. She reminded him of the child who had belonged to his London neighbours. Their garden had adjoined him, part of the fencing was down, and the child, a girl, would come through, walk up to the tall, uncurtained windows of Somerville's study and stare in. If he went and sat in the garden, she came to stand a few yards away from his chair, saying nothing, asking no questions, only staring, until he felt that he could neither move nor breathe, he had stayed indoors and bought a blind and rammed it down hard in the child's face, loathing it. He realized, one day, how he loathed it, and was overcome with disgust at himself, and with guilt, too, for the child did not trouble him, it made no noise, touched nothing. Only came up to his window and stared, still-faced.

In the end, he had sold the house.

"My Gran's on the way out."

"Your . . .?"

"Gran — *you* know her, you've seen her, in the shop. Everybody knows her."

"No."

"She lives with us. Well, she did. They've had to take her now, though, into the hospital at Cittingham. We couldn't stand it."

She sat down on the terrace, her long thin legs sprawling out from under the yellow dress.

"I didn't think it'd bother me, not at all. Well — she's old, everybody dies when they're old, don't they? Everybody has to. Only when you go and see her you feel awful. When they ring the bell for the end of visiting, she starts pushing back the covers, you know, trying to get out of bed. 'Where's me clothes, where's me clothes,' she says. They had to hold her down, the time I went. That makes you feel awful, you coming out of there and just carrying on, everything carrying on and her staying in the hospital to die. Especially in this weather. It makes it seem worse, somehow, everything seems as though it's more living, doesn't it, in the sun?"

Somerville thought, do not tell me this, it has nothing to do with me, I want to hear nothing of your grandmother. I have thought of all that, gone through all those questions and solved them, years ago, the problems of living and dying. It is sealed and packed away, that knowledge. I will not listen to you. It is nothing to me.

> Yesterday we dug Lewis Higton out. I mean dead. He was frozen stiff, he'd gone in up to the chest... We went back for him. But we dug him out and he was dead... We shouldn't have dug him out, should we, we should have left him there, just left him.

"It's funny about my Gran. I mean, she's old, she's gone seventy, and she's a bit funny, you know, about some things. You've to be careful what you say to Gran. But she was the only one of them who didn't go on and on at me about this."

This.

"She just gave me a look, you know. One look. You'd have thought she'd be worse than anyone, wouldn't you? I did. Really shocked, that's what I thought she'd be. Well it's that generation, isn't it? It's what you'd expect. But it wasn't her at all, it was them, they were the ones. My God! *She* went to bed for the whole day, she had hysterics, you'd have thought it was her that'd caught again. And my brother, he was the same. And that's a laugh, as well, if you knew what he was like himself in that direction. You can't tell me. No, it was only Gran that didn't bother. I went to see her yesterday. She looks all shrunk up, and she kept calling me Cissy, as well — that's my Aunt Cissy, the one that died. She thought I was her daughter, only young again. Her mind's gone all confused. That really upset me."

Somerville began to hear her voice as though from far away, it went on and he heard it and yet did not hear it, he ceased to listen. It was almost dark. The drawing-room lamps threw long fingers of light on to the terrace.

"It started in her womb, they said, so far as they could tell anyway. I suppose it'll just creep all over her."

He thought, she is not here. I can close my eyes and ears and then she does not exist in this world. Everything is the same. *She is not here.*

"It's a terrible thing, I think, cancer, it's like a sort of hand, isn't it, spreading out inside you. That's what it's like."

"The crab," he said distantly. "Cancer the crab."

She turned her head and he closed his eyes again at once, not wanting to be seen by her, not wanting his secrets known. *She is not here.*

"I tell you what else, as well. I found out something from my Gran, today. I found out that it happened to them."

Her voice was thick with satisfaction.

"They had to get married because of our Dave. It happened to them! You'd have thought I was the first and last, you'd have thought they never knew anyone so bad, the way they went on at me. Only I know all about it now, don't I? My Gran told me. She thought I was my Aunt Cissy, she started talking all about it, telling me, I couldn't believe it, not at first. Well, you can't be sure of everything she says now, I told you, not with the injections they give her. Only in the end I did believe it. And do you know what I did? I went home and I went in that kitchen and I just asked them, I just said it, out loud, I said, it happened to you, didn't it, only you never told me, you had our Dave like that, just the same, everything the same, and the only difference is you got wed and I'm not, that's all. I stood there and said it. They were having sardine salad for tea, all sitting there. My hands were shaking, you know, all trembling. I didn't care though, not about any of them."

Somerville half-opened his eyes. She was smiling, looking away across the garden.

She said, "That did for them."

He began to think about it, the scene in the kitchen at the back of the grocer's shop, sardine salad on white plates, the face of the girl, and then was horrified at finding himself interested at all in what she said. He wanted to wave his arms at her again, to shout, why do you come here, why do you talk to me, *why*? For she spoke as though she had always been this familiar, as if they inhabited the same world.

"It upset me, seeing my Gran in the hospital. I didn't expect it to. Not so much as that."

He thought in panic, she will come here again and again, there will be nothing I can do, she will come and bring the child and the child will know me, she will come here. I shall have to move away.

"I can't talk about it to them. I can't say anything about any of it."

> Then high above his head they placed
> a golden banner and let the waves bear him
> bequeathed him to the sea.

But now he had a terrible image of the old woman in a hospital bed, struggling to get up, pushing back the blankets, struggling against such a commonplace, public death. "Where's me clothes? Where's me clothes?"

"They've had to put her in a room by herself now. She was with all the others, you know, in the general ward, but they've put her on her own now, because of the smell. That was why they couldn't stand it at home. That's the worst of it, isn't it, the way it smells?"

> We shouldn't have dug him out, should we, we should have left him there, just left him . . .

Then he remembered, he saw Barton, exactly as he was. Not Barton the ghost, Barton of the photograph. Barton. The colour of his eyes and hair, the precise mould of flesh over bone. Barton, hands in pockets, shaking his head.

"Look at that!"

A yard away, the hedgehog was drinking from the blue saucer.

He would say, quite firmly, you must not come here, I do not wish to see you, I do not wish to have any visitors. For he began to imagine how it would be, summer merging into autumn and winter, and then she would bring the child up here, crying and crawling, and it would be too cold for the terrace by then, he would have gone inside the house, and she would come there to find him. He wondered how many of the others already knew that she had been up here, to whom she had talked about him, about the way he lived.

He felt helpless. He realized that he himself had spoken almost nothing, half a dozen disconnected sentences, in his anxiety to be rid of her. She had talked.

You must not come here. I have always been alone. I will be alone now. You have nothing to do with me.

He walked up and down the garden in the early morning, rehearsing phrases. I bought this house, gave up my public life . . . I do not wish to see you, to see anyone.

The rose Sanders White had climbed and spread up and along the whole of the west wall, and now it was tumbling over the other side. When he came here, it had been nothing, a few thin, stray branches. In the autumn, he would have to cut it hard back. Or perhaps not. Perhaps leave it, let it riot as it chose. He was certain, from time to time, that he should do this, should simply leave the garden, apart from the ugliest of the weeds and the cutting of the grass. For perhaps to be a gardener was not an honourable thing, perhaps he ought not to impose his own private, artificial order, upon the land.

He walked about for a long time, soothed by the familiar argument, for he knew down which path this and that and that extension of it led, knew the various conclusions. He turned his back upon Sanders White and looked ahead, into the dark green, watery light, between the beech trees.

But it was not true that no one at all had ever been here. His sister had been.

Even now, even four years afterwards, he remembered the feeling he had had, on waking, the knowledge that someone else had slept under his roof, that his sister was breathing up the air in a room two floors below, the sudden panic. He had run out of the house and down the path to the lake, pushing his arms out in wide circles through the air, trying to get away. There had been a buzzing noise within his head, a confusion, he had felt, for the only time since coming here, that he did not have any hold upon himself, that he was spread about, his skin could not contain him. His sister had come, someone was here who shared his blood and knew about his past, someone who spoke of rights and duties, awakening in him the old, childish feeling of threat and dread.

He shook his head. The garden was empty, the leaves rustling about against one another, inside the beech copse.

Once, he had said to Barton, "I hate my sister." It was the first year they had met, the first time they had gone abroad on holiday.

"I hate my sister!"

They had been standing in the pink- and lemon-coloured early morning, on a hill above Assisi. Barton's face, as he turned slowly and looked up at him, had been smooth and pale with a kind of horror at the words, his skin seemed to be pulled more tightly across the bones. Below them, the beautiful roof-tops of the town, rose- and sand- and slate-sea-coloured in the southern sun.

"I hate my sister!"

"You can't say that!" Barton had stood up. "You *cannot* say that!" But he spoke more quietly than ever, so that Somerville had not recognized anger, had laughed.

"Oh, I can! I know her, I've spent a good deal of my life with her. I can say it. 'I hate my sister!'"

Then, Barton had simply walked away from him, on and on down the hill, not pausing or looking back, had vanished into the town. Later, towards the evening, Somerville had found him, sitting on the steps of a church. They did not yet have any place to stay. Nothing had been said about the morning, nothing. He had not understood, Barton continued to bewilder and at times to frighten him. His own sister had not been mentioned again.

Afterwards, he knew Barton, knew everything about him, afterwards, they grew older. He learned that Barton never spoke grandiosely, as the others did, about humanity, about the general good, about society, but that he cared for those people he knew, and above all, cared about family, the ties of blood, for the closeness of mother and sister, cousin and grandfather and aunt, in a way Somerville could not begin to understand. Somerville, who hated the claustrophobic feeling of shared blood and bone, hated to look in his mirror and see "the family nose". He said, I am alone, I am alone, my skin is a bag containing everything of me, and outside there is nothing, no one who has anything to do with me.

As a small child, he had gone about saying that he had not been born, as others were. One moment, there had been a world without him, the next, he had simply been altogether there. In adult life, he recognized the depth of his longing for this to be true. He felt pried upon, and lessened, remembering that he shared a relationship of flesh with others.

"I hate my sister!"

Barton, he had jealously thought, Barton and his sister were too close, they wrote letters and sent one another cards, each sought out small, ridiculous trophies and tokens for the other, they shared jokes and spoke a private language, thought one another's thoughts. So that, over the years, he had wondered which of them he hated most, his own, or Barton's sister.

Except that Barton knew and laughed and shook his head, mocking him. And he was a little reassured, seeing that in any case Barton was the same with all the others, with the most distant members of that enormous family.

"I hate my sister!"

But his sister had come. She had not written him any letter, knowing, perhaps, if she knew anything of him at all, that he would find time to make some excuse, to go away, that he might even fail to open the envelope at all. She had not written, therefore. He had not seen her for almost eleven years. She had come, driven up to the house one afternoon in September, by taxi from Cittingham station. She had arrived.

Because she had grown much fatter, not thinner, with age, she no longer looked very much like him. Except for the nose, "the family nose".

"And *haven't* you looked after yourself? *Haven't* you made yourself comfortable?"

He had forgotten it and now remembered, the way she talked, he heard her voice sounding down his childhood. She went about the house, his house, in and out of rooms, stroking the furniture, lifting this and that, the expert eye valuing.

"Oh yes, it is only what I would have expected of you, it is entirely typical. *Haven't* you got just what you wanted!"

She had turned suddenly to face him, standing by the drawing-room windows, so that the incoming light flattened her features even more, gave her a bland, characterless look, he could attribute no past to her, no experience. Though he could imagine her in the shop, driving a bargain over an occasional table, talking very fast and assuredly about silver, selling a bad steel engraving to a fool.

Once, he had been there, had gone right up to the window of her shop, peered in, at lustre-ware jugs on oak dressers, at corner cabinets full of air-twist stems, at screens and stools and headed cushions. Even standing outside, he had been able to smell the smell of the shop, and to imagine his sister within it, moving her hands about as she talked, catching sight of herself in a cheval mirror, of "the family nose", and looking away, for she was a woman embarrassed by herself. She wore clothes which did not suit her, roughly textured tweeds or busy patterns on dark silk, with small feathered or fruited hats. He had been passing through the town on his way to some conference and remembered that she lived there, had driven about looking for the shop. But after having seen it, he had gone away at once, not liking this place, not wanting to meet her.

"You had better come and take what is yours away," she had said that day. "It is all there, everything is left. You had better come down for a day."

Somerville stared.

"There are only the two of us, we see nothing of one another. Well then, you had better get it over with, come and take away what is yours, of the family property."

Outside, the beech leaves were drifting up the lawn in the wind, piling softly against the rose-red brick of the house.

"*The family property*."

He had wanted to kill her, to make her disappear, this thick flat-faced woman in his house, his room. His sister.

He said, "I want none of it, you must do as you think best, it is your own affair. I have everything here, there is nothing at all I would possibly want."

"The house is sold. I took it upon myself to do that."

He shrugged.

"You had better have what is yours by right, I wish to do what is correct. There are only the two of us. You should come down and choose."

"No."

There were things he remembered suddenly, from the house in Kent, things he had touched and stared at and known daily, through his childhood, the patterns upon carpets, the knobs on particular chairs, things he did not wish to see again.

"I have everything I want here."

She began to look about her again, the keeper of the antique shop, so that Somerville wanted to hide things, to shut the doors of cupboards and mask over the glass, to close the lids of his own eyes.

"Well, I am not surprised by you, whatever others may think. You behave strangely as you have always behaved strangely. Nothing you did has ever startled *me*."

He had tried to say that he did not care, that he wanted her to feel nothing towards him at all, to put him out of her mind, but he could only make half-remarks, only repeat, "I have everything. There is nothing I would have."

She had stayed for another day, and he had scarcely been able to bear it, to bear the smell of her about the house, to hear the movement of silk stocking against silk stocking on her thighs as she walked.

She had said, "You should knock down that wall, make this drawing-room longer."

"You should pave that side lawn, neaten things off, save yourself trouble."

"You should have these things properly insured."

"You have done well for yourself. But then, you have had no responsibilities, no family cares." Though her own husband had died, before the war, before they had been married a year, had left no children, no trace of himself upon her.

She said, "Do you remember that man you once knew? That man Barton?"

When she left, he had gone up to her bedroom and found hairs on the dressing table, pale beige hairs, dry and curling at the corners like dead things. His hands had been trembling.

Every day for weeks afterwards, he had woken and heard the wind, the leaves rattling down, and been lifted up by his sense of new freedom, and the emptiness of the house, by the sight of his books on the shelves and of Barton's charcoal drawings framed in rows upon the walls, by the long tunnel of cool air down between the beech trees leading to the lake. He had thought, I am here, I am myself, I have everything. Nobody shall come.

That is what he would say then, to the girl, what he would tell her.

"You must not come here again. No one shall come."

She said, "What happened to the hedgehog, then?"

She was wearing the same yellow dress, puffed out over her stomach, the same expression of face, pert and world-weary.

Somerville straightened his back slowly, sucked a rose-thorn out of his thumb, said you are not to come here, I will not speak to you, you are to go away, summoning up words inside himself, staying silent.

"There was one I saw on the road the other day, all squashed up where a car had hit it. They're not very bright are they, hedgehogs?"

His head thundered, in his anxiety, he felt violently protective towards the hedgehog, desperate to make her understand everything about them, to know what he knew. He began to speak anxiously. "It is a defence, they curl up — it's their spines — they sense danger and roll up at once . . . it is to protect themselves, it is . . ." He lifted a hand hopelessly, imagining the small body burst open, the stumpy, inquisitive nose, upon the gravel road. "How can you expect them to know of cars and lorries, of the speed and power of the engine? How should they know that?"

She had settled herself on the terrace, legs like those of a wooden doll, stuck out straight in front of her.

"Oh, no. They're little vermin though, aren't they? I mean, they're very nice, pretty and that, I like them. But they're vermin, all the same."

"*No!*"

"They suck the milk from cows in the fields at night. Did you know that?"

He had reached her and now was pacing up and down the terrace. He wondered how he would be now, trying to address some meeting, to give a public lecture, for he could not make the words jell together and come clearly out of his mouth, could not use them in a neat, clear line to express his thoughts. He saw them marshalled like rows of soldiers, but the soldiers were felled by cannon, there was a confusion, blood and mess and smoke, a tremendous noise. He breathed in deeply, held the breath. He said, "The hedgehog is the most maligned, the most misunderstood animal . . . it . . . listen . . . the *lies* told about . . ."

"Well, what about the fruit then? They like fruit, hedgehogs do, they eat that. People might be right about the fruit."

"No. They only eat fruit when they are obliged to, when there is nothing else at all. Hedgehogs are flesh eaters, hunting animals, destroyers of insects and snails and garden pests. Even of snakes. Did you know that the hedgehog is almost entirely resistant to the poison of a snake? Did you know that?"

She drummed her heels impatiently upon the terrace, like a child. "What about the *fruit*, why couldn't they carry it that way, if they wanted it? I don't see why they mightn't."

He took up a piece of stone and began furiously to make marks upon the terrace. "These are the spines, stiff, all down the back, all over the skin . . . but when the hedgehog rolls over, *if* it does, then the back muscle relaxes, and the spines just go loose, they fold over like . . . No, no, can't you see? It would be impossible, no matter what the fruit. A man would have to hold the animal and press an apple down on to one of the spines from above, he . . . No, it is simply another lie, a lie everyone tells. It could not be *done* in that way."

Somerville heard the echo of his own voice, almost hysterical.

"It could not be *done*!"

"Not even if they wanted the fruit."

"No."

"And they don't?"

"No."

The willow warbler started up, and a thrush from the bushes. Somerville looked down at his own hands, at the faint, tobacco-coloured freckles between his thin fingers, at the marks made with his bit of stone upon the paving.

"You know a lot, I must say. About hedgehogs. You do know an awful lot."

He wondered whether she were laughing at him.

"I suppose that's what it's like though, living up here, in this place, all on your own, you get interested in funny things like that, you get carried away, don't you?"

He stood up awkwardly. "Yes." He thought, I should not have begun to speak to her, I do not wish her to come here. Except that he had felt it important, he had spent so long, watching the hedgehog, it distressed him beyond bearing to hear the old, repeated lies.

"You ought to write a book about it, then. Be something for you to do, wouldn't it? Take your mind off things."

Things . . .

He said, "I am very happy . . . I am . . . I have everything here."

"Still . . ."

She leaned back against the wall, closing her eyes, Somerville watched and the anxiety began to rise in him again, seeing the patch of yellow dress against the rose-red brick. When she arrived, he had been about to go down to the lake, he wanted to smell the close, sweet soil-smell, down between the beeches, to see the water.

"It's a pull now, coming up that hill. I really noticed it tonight. It's a pull on my back."

He stood, uncertain, silent.

"It's lovely and warm against this wall. Lovely. Only I really did notice it, walking up. It's like having something in a sack tied round you, that's what it's like. Like being a cow."

The thrush had moved nearer, to the roof of the garden shed.

"It's about time it was over and done with, that's what. I'm about ready for that, I can tell you. And that's another thing, we've had all *that* again tonight, as if I'm not sick of it — that's another reason I had to get out of the house. You wouldn't think I'd already told them, would you, over and over. They've got no respect for me, no respect for my mind, have they, they think they can just argue and order me about and I'll change it to suit them, do just what they want."

Her eyes were still closed, she talked on and on, as easily as a child, relaxed against the wall.

"'*We'll* look after it, *we'll* have it here, keep it, the both of you,' that's how they go on. 'You ought to let things like this stay in the family, it's got nothing to do with strangers, you listen to what we say, we know, we're older than you, we know what's best. We'll have the baby and you, you'll live here, just the same. That's what you *ought* to do, what's right, and anything else in your head is wicked, it's unnatural.'"

She opened her eyes. "There was Mrs Mason's girl, you know her — Mrs Mason up at the bungalow? Well, her daughter had a little girl, that Sally, and she wasn't married, and she brought it home you see, lived with her mother and father, they all lived together. Until she upped and married someone else in the finish and they've gone elsewhere now. It was all one big happy family though, till then. Catch me!"

She glanced down at the puffed-out yellow dress. "It'll be over and done with and gone. There's plenty of people waiting for babies, aren't there, I know all about it, plenty of people like that and welcome, in this world."

Somerville felt dazed, standing in the evening sunlight, felt lightheaded. He thought, I know nothing, understand nothing — and looked at the girl in amazement and dread.

His head was full of pictures, columns of numbers and snatches from half-remembered tunes, full of the sound of dead voices, full of images — nothing. He felt that he might blow suddenly away, like one of the brown curls of beech leaf on the terrace in October, leaving no trace.

She said, "I've got it all worked out."

He would say, I do not wish to see you again, or talk to you, I do not wish you to visit me.

But a fortnight went by and the girl did not come again. Somerville cut the blooms of pink and red and orange roses and crammed them into bowls and vases in all the rooms of the house, the air was heavy with the smell of roses, and in the copse the leaves of the beech trees yellowed in the heat.

A picture came into his mind, and stayed with him through those hot days of July, of his mother, who had been ill with this or that indefinable complaint, for most of the summers of his childhood. He saw her, from the window-bench on which he was sitting, half-propped upon fat pillows and turning her head restlessly against them, in the bed. Beyond this window there had been a garden, with too much rockery and flat lawn and privet hedge, and a cedar tree standing squat in the middle of its own black shadows.

"How *boring* the summer is!" his mother said, "and this heat, glaring on and on. How I hate the summer!"

He had stared at her and been amazed, and when

he had looked back across the garden, it was to see everything differently, he tried on his mother's eyes as though they were spectacles, he thought her thoughts. "How *boring* the summer is!" But the summer became his favourite time, then, for it had taken him only a short while to perceive the truth about his own mother, and then he could not bear to stay with her, could not bear the languid, dissatisfied voice, though he was obliged to bear it, for she demanded his company.

Now, he thought, I have no need to remember that, I am an ageing man, I am able to do what *I* choose, in my own house, my own garden. I have everything. He began to get up even earlier in the mornings, while a thin mist still clung on the air between the trees, and sat on the terrace reading — Beowulf and Skelton and the political novels of Trollope, the grey-bound book of Japanese poetry, he thought that he would read everything Barton had ever given to him.

The hedgehog, too, was often about at this time, trailing sleepily away over the lawn, or snuffling in the mulch underneath the roses for a snail.

But it was an evening, when he came back up the path from the lake and remembered the lemon-yellow dress. He stopped dead, looking up towards the house. He thought, the child is born and the grandmother is dead and I am here, I am as I choose to be, I have everything. I am a wicked man.

The following day he walked down the hill to the village.

"Oh, they talk about *you*, don't they? You're like the weather, you are, always good for a chat."

So that now, he felt them staring at him, he walked along the dull main street and the windows of the houses were like eyes.

"It's all I can do just to keep going, I can tell you that, it's about all I can do, I've wondered if I ever would manage it, these past few weeks. Leave her, the doctor says, don't fuss her, just leave her be, don't take any notice. How am I supposed to do that? It upsets me, it really does, watching her. She does everything for it, feeds it, bathes it and it might be a lump of putty, the way she looks, Mrs Haswell, it might just be a lump of putty. It's not natural that, is it? I can't make her out and there's something wrong, whatever he says. And then that hospital, night after night, and you wonder when *that'll* end, and half the time she doesn't even know us, you see, when we go, doesn't even know who we are. I'm just about up to here, what with that and the way she is, over that baby. It's about all I can do, just to carry on. It is."

In the end, Somerville came out of the shop without speaking at all, he left his grocery list on the counter and pushed his way out into the hard sunlight of the street, trying to get his breath, wishing that he had not heard the voice of the girl's mother, had not discovered about the old woman, still dying in hospital, and about the girl who fed and bathed her child and looked at it as though it were a lump of putty. They were both silent as he went so abruptly out, the girl's mother staring at him, fat and hostile in a blue nylon overall, the customer contemptuous, bored, he felt tainted by their staring and their voices, by the mess of other people's lives.

The heat shimmered just above the roadway, as he walked back up the hill.

Then, he went inside the house and was restless as he had never been here before, going from room to room and hearing the silence, fiddling with the roses in their bowls. He thought, I should write a book, about the hedgehog, do what she told me, I would answer all their questions, make some use of my own knowledge, of those months of observation. I should justify my life.

"Give you something to do, wouldn't it, take your mind off things . . ."

Things.

He went to his desk. He would sort out all the notes he had made, on scraps of paper and in diaries, he would begin.

At the back of the desk, he found again the unopened letter. He thought, the child is born and is not wanted, the old woman is dying. He read, "September 2. Hedgehog ate milky custard from saucer (sweet). Fish later. V. cold morning and evening. Hibernation?"

> I can't write, not much, I can't hold the pen . . . only thought you'd care to know about Higton. He played the piano, didn't he? The one in your rooms . . . We shouldn't have dug him out, should we, we should have left him there, just left him . . .

Somerville walked out of the house on to the terrace, and the heat came up from the flagstones like the blast of an oven, full in his face. The shadows were hard and black-edged. Nothing moved.

He thought, I have everything here, no one shall come. I have everything. I am a wicked man.

It was years since he had ridden in a bus. He had forgotten how the seats smelled, made hot by the sun through glass, and the rough white tickets that came whirring out of the machine. He had forgotten how close the other people were, and how much they stared. He was like a man newly released from years of imprisonment. When he got off the bus, in the main street of Cittingham, he had no idea in which direction to go, the rush of the cars confused him. Only Woolworths looked the same, the lettering of the sign, gold on red, as it had always been. He stood for some time, in the doorway of Woolworths, feeling safe.

Having made his decision, early that morning, he had thought little about it. It was simply clear to him that he had a duty to come to this place, to see what he ought to see. If he did not, his life would sour like the roots of a plant, left for too long in an old pot. He was guilty of too much happiness.

He had known what kind of building the hospital would be, the shape of each block, like so many cut-off squares of cake, set down at angles to one another, had known about the buff colour of the outside paint and the green of the inside corridors. He knew how it would smell and the sounds he would hear, of metal against enamel and the shriek of wheelchair rubbers upon polished floors.

Walking up the driveway of this building, his bowels turned in a moment of fear, he thought of the beds hidden claustrophobically behind screens, and the massed petals of hothouse flowers. But he had not thought of anything else, beyond these softly swinging doors, did not know what he was to say.

"Her name is Mrs . . .?"

Oh, God. He tried to picture the letters of the name, written above the village shop.

T-R-

T-A . . .

T-R-A-B . . .

"Trabe."

"Mrs Trabe? And you are?"

He stared.

"Your *name*?"

Somerville leaned his hands on the edge of the desk, pushed his face forward, he said desperately, "My name is Somerville, I am . . . I am her brother. The brother of Mrs Trabe . . . she has cancer . . . she is in a room alone . . . I am . . ."

The wasp began to vibrate on the glass.

"You are Mrs Trabe's *brother*? You have come some distance? But why did you not tell me that to begin with?"

Because I am afraid, he would have said, because I am a liar, for I do not know why I have come here . . .

"This way . . ."

"Mrs Trabe? Wake up, dearie, come along, let's have you sitting up just a little bit, make you nice and comfy. Let's wipe your mouth. Mrs Trabe?"

The room smelled hot and septic.

"Here's your brother, Mrs Trabe." She bent down very

close to the old woman's ear. "*Your brother*. Here's your brother come to see you."

There were bones and skin and glistening eyes. No flesh.

"Not too long, now, I can't give you too long, not in the morning, however far you've come. *It's your brother, dear.* Don't expect too much, Mr Somerville. Don't expect too much."

The eyes opened, very dark and glassy, like marbles under water, set in the sockets of the face. Somerville stood back, hands locked inside his pockets, smelled the suppurating smell. Then the neck poked forward, the skin unfolding like a tortoise. She said, "It's our John," and then laughed, or coughed, terrifying him.

"I told them, didn't I?" The eyes slid away and then back again to his face. "I told them. I said, he'll come, you wait, I know him. He'll come. I told them. It was her, she was the one, trying to make out you were dead. She's never liked us, not really. But I told them . . ."

Somerville ran.

"We do what we can, Mr Somerville. You do see how it is? We do what we can."

She had caught up with him, at the glass door of the entrance hall, blocked his way out.

"It can't be long. I'm sorry to have to tell you that."

Tell me nothing, he thought. Do not speak to me.

"I'm glad she's seen you. It's always best, isn't it, always nice, when everyone can get to see them, all the relatives. I am glad. She recognized you, didn't she? Knew you straight away. She's not always done that, you know, not just lately. I'm sorry to have to tell you that."

She walked with him out of the glass doors, ushered him to the top of the drive, spoke to him of the weather and of how they did their best for his sister, so that it seemed that he had, after all, mysteriously kept the rules and won the game, had found favour.

The air in the streets was thick with the fumes of traffic, so that the difference between this world and his own seemed to be entirely one of good and evil smells, good and evil noises.

In the bus his hand shook violently, he spilled the fare money in between the dusty treads of the floor.

He had told a lie and gained access to the room of a dying old woman who was not known to him, he had cheated and won, and she had taken him for her dead brother.

He began to weep, the other passengers stared at him and a fat woman moved from his side, to a seat further up the vehicle in the opposite aisle.

Walking up the drive towards the rose-red house, it seemed to him that there was, after all, no answer, and he was bewildered, for he had made the terrible journey because he expected to find one, to have the problem solved. Barton would have known what to do, would have sat quietly in the sun and shaken his head, Barton would have told him the answer. So he relied, then, upon a man who had been twenty-five years dead?

The flower-bed beneath the drawing-room windows blazed with mesembryanthemums, flat and bright as medallions in the mid-day sun.

But I am here, I have this, I have everything, Somerville thought. Nothing is changed. No one shall come to trouble me.

Inside the front door, on the mat, lay a second letter.

Just after dawn, he woke from the last of the nightmares and got up, he could no longer bear the pictures that lay in wait behind his closed eyelids.

Out on the lawn, the early sun glinted silver as a razor between the grass-blades. The air smelled damp.

Gradually he felt calmer, his hand no longer shook, holding the mug of coffee. He thought of the lake.

When he emerged from the green tunnel of beeches, he saw that the grass around the margin of the water beside the path had already been disturbed, the footprints lay dark as blood-stains in the dew. He stood, listening, looking out across the water. Down here, it was still quite cold.

After a time, he began to walk slowly around the edge of the lake.

He found the body of the baby in a hollow at the base of one of the trees. She had scarcely bothered to conceal it, only cursorily covered the face with handfuls of leaves and grass. The torn ends were still wet and green with the sap.

Somerville found that he was neither surprised nor appalled, only certain, at once, that he must do something, and of what it should be. There were no marks upon the child, only the flesh was faintly blue-white, about the face and throat, the eyelids a little swollen.

She would have known that before long he would come down here, that he was the most likely person to discover it. He felt curiously proud, that she had trusted him. He wondered how distressed she was, where she was, now.

On the far side of the lake there was the wooden shed, though he had scarcely been into it since coming here, he had no idea in what condition the rowing boat was by now, whether it had rotted altogether from seeping damp and disuse.

For a moment, he stood, looking down at the body under its scattering of leaves. It occurred to him that someone else might come here, the boys she had told him about, who poached his fish from the lake. He carried the baby over to the shed. It felt limp and strangely heavy and when the back of his hand brushed against its face, the flesh was cold to his touch. He wondered what she had done.

After that, he went back up to the house, and he felt nervous, and excited, too, wanting to do anything in order to make a pattern, he was following a chart, laid out in his head.

Behind the plant pots in the toolshed, he found the largest of the wooden trugs, and sawed the handle carefully off at each end. The wooden slats seemed plaited tightly enough, overlapping from end to end, he thought that it would do. In the linen cupboard of the house, he found a freshly laundered cotton pillowcase.

The sun was much higher, and the mesembryan-themums had already unfolded. When he reached the lake again, the dew was dry, and the water gleamed like brass at the rim.

Lifting the child up and wrapping it, laying it in the wooden trug, he felt his heart begin to race, for fear anyone should come before he were finished. But it was not out of any sense of guilt.

Once, there had been a gravel slope running down from the shed to the edge of the water, but now it was thickly overgrown, so that he could scarcely drag the boat through the grass and weeds and protruding tree roots. The oars lay in the bottom, tangled with dust and the old webs of spiders, woven to and fro. At the edge, he stepped inside and moved his feet about, walked from end to end, tested the wooden seat. It was a small lake, he thought that the boat would take him to the centre of it and back again, and if it did not, the water was still, he could swim.

He set the basket, into which the baby's body exactly fitted, in the bottom of the boat.

For a moment, he thought he had forgotten how to row, he could not remember which way to fit his hands round the oars. They had spent long afternoons of each summer on the river. But then, Barton had always rowed.

Barton.

Now, there were other people, the girl mattered to him, and the old woman in the hospital bed and the dead child. He thought, I am doing what I can.

In the centre of the lake, he let the oars rest. The water went still. All around him, the beech trees, lime-yellow where the sun shone through them, and dark at the heart, and between them he could see the rose-red house. Nothing moved.

From his breast-pocket, Somerville took the two unopened letters, and laid them in the trug, at the side of the baby in the white pillow-case. When he lowered it over the side, it touched the water without a splash, hovered for a second, and then began to glide almost imperceptibly away from him.

At once, he began to turn the rowing boat around.

When he had almost reached the edge again, he looked back. The trug was almost out of sight, sinking lower and lower in the water, and still moving away. He waited until it had completely disappeared.

In the house behind the village shop, the girl moved quietly about her room, emptying drawers and wardrobes, filling a suitcase. It was a little after six o'clock. She worked methodically, her thoughts vague. She had planned everything, long before.

Somerville made a fresh pot of coffee and took it out on to the terrace. He began to read. But in a little while, he saw that the hedgehog had come over the lawn, towards the blue saucer, so that he laid down his book carefully and began to watch it.

Nothing troubled him.

Author's Afterword

The debt writers owe to their sources of inspiration cannot always be acknowledged, simply because it is not always possible to trace back to that source. But the debt I owe to the work of Benjamin Britten is crystal clear to me, and clearest of all in the case of *The Albatross.* Without the dramatic impact upon me of Britten's music, as well as his personality and the place in which he worked, together with some of the books and ideas that had in their turn inspired him, I would not have written the book at all — and that holds good for at least another two of my novels, *Strange Meeting* and *The Bird of Night.* My imaginative life and my inner self would have been very different and greatly impoverished if I had not been so overwhelmingly affected by Britten.

I first heard his music the "Sea Interludes" from the opera *Peter Grimes* when I was still at school, and it made a startling impact upon me, as few other things in my life have done, so that I still remember in vivid detail the room in which I was sitting, even the design on the cover of the file on my knee. In part, the music reminded me of the bleak North Sea coast beside which I was born and where I had lived until a few months before — and which, in my Midlands city sixth form, I desperately missed. But the impact went much deeper, and I became completely obsessed by the music and the story behind *Peter Grimes* — and so, gradually, by the rest of Britten's life and work.

But it was not until twelve years later that I finally made my first pilgrimage to the small Suffolk seaside town of Aldeburgh, where Britten lived and worked and which pervaded his imaginative life. At once, I fell under its spell both as it was in reality, and as that other Aldeburgh, whose spirit permeates the music.

Once there, it was only a matter of time before I wrote about it and before the real and the imaginary Aldeburgh merged in my own work. So, the Heype of *The Albatross* is Aldeburgh; that coast is the Suffolk coast — and yet, of course, because the book is my fiction the two are entirely different.

I do not know, otherwise, where the story and the characters of *The Albatross* came from; I know only that the book wrote itself. All the best writing does that — and by "the best" I mean that which comes from the deepest depths of the self and speaks the truth and could be in no way other than it is. I began to make a few notes while I was still staying in Suffolk that first winter, and when I started writing (on a train, going between London and Warwickshire!) the story unwound itself from me like a thread and knitted itself together into paragraphs before my astonished eyes. I felt as if I were having no part of it, as if I were taking down dictation from some inner voice. That has happened just a few times in the course of my writing life. It is an awesome experience.

What *The Albatross* is about is pretty plain; it is about the misfit, the odd, the simple, the strange one in the midst of the rest of ordinary humanity, and about the power of love and pure goodness, shining through all manner of human exteriors. It is about possessiveness and cruelty and oppression, about fear and pride. Duncan is one of God's fools. Old Beatty is one of His saints. Yet both are in some way outside of and outcasts from society. Hilda Pike's wrongs are understandable, though not excusable.

Beyond the people, the story is about a place — a place which has as strong a character as any of the human figures — about the coast, the sea and its power and the little fishing town that has grown up at its edge in subservience to it, about the narrow, dark lanes and the wide East Anglian skies, the boats, the raging elements — all those things that I found in Aldeburgh which had been so intimate a part of my childhood and which I had rediscovered again imaginatively through Britten's music.

Susan Hill, 1988

ISIS
LARGE PRINT

FICTION

Phyllis Shand Allfrey	**The Orchid House**
Julian Barnes	**A History of the world in 10 ½ Chapters (A)**
Nina Bawden	**A Woman of My Age**
Charlotte Bingham	**At Home**
Charlotte Bingham	**By Invitation**
Melvyn Bragg	**The Hired Man**
John Braine	**Room at the Top**
Anita Brookner	**Providence**
Pearl S Buck	**The Good Earth**
Robertson Davies	**Murther and Walking Spirits**
Penelope Fitzgerald	**The Beginning of Spring**
Rumer Godden	**An Episode of Sparrows**
Georgette Heyer	**The Quiet Gentleman**
Georgette Heyer	**The Reluctant Widow**
Susan Hill	**I'm the King of the Castle**

(A) Large Print books also available in Audio

FICTION

Thomas Keneally	**Flying Hero Class (A)**
Penelope Lively	**City of the Mind**
David Lodge	**Paradise News**
Colleen McCullough	**Tim**
Ian McEwan	**The Child in Time**
Wolf Mankowitz	**A Kid for Two Farthings**
Gabriel Garcia Marquez	**One Hundred Years of Solitude**
Sue Miller	**For Love**
Geoffrey Morgan	**Tea With Mr Timothy**
Iris Murdoch	**Under the Net**
Anthony Powell	**The Fisher King**
Marjorie Quarton	**One Dog, His Man and His Trials**
Colin Thubron	**Falling (A)**
J R R Tolkien	**The Hobbit**
Edith Wharton	**The Age of Innocence**
Virginia Woolf	**Orlando**

(A) Large Print books also available in Audio

SHORT STORIES

Thomas Godfrey	**Country House Murders, Volume 2**
Thomas Godfrey	**Country House Murders, Volume 3**
M R James	**Ghost Stories of An Antiquary (A)**
Stephen King	**Night Shift**
Louis L'Amour	**The Outlaws of Mesquite**

HUMOUR

Douglas Adams	**Mostly Harmless**
Daphne du Maurier	**Rule Britannia**
Terry Pratchett	**Equal Rites**
David Renwick	**One Foot in the Grave**
Tom Sharpe	**Ancestral Vices**
Tom Sharpe	**The Great Pursuit**

(A) Large Print books also available in Audio

THRILLERS, CRIME AND ADVENTURE

THRILLERS, CRIME AND ADVENTURE

Stephen King	**Carrie**
Stephen King	**'Salem's Lot**
Elmore Leonard	**Get Shorty**
Elmore Leonard	**Maximum Bob**
Elmore Leonard	**Pronto**
Elmore Leonard	**Rum Punch**
Elmore Leonard	**The Switch**
Elmore Leonard	**Unknown Man No. 89**
Ed McBain	**Kiss**
Sara Paretsky	**Deadlock**
Sara Paretsky	**Guardian Angel**
Alan Plater	**The Beiderbecke Connection**
Mickey Spillane	**The Killing Man**
Mickey Spillane	**The Twisted Thing**
Arthur Upfield	**The Bone is Pointed**
Arthur Upfield	**The Lake Frome Monster**
Arthur Upfield	**The Sands of Windee (A)**
Owen Wister	**The Virginian**

(A) Large Print books available in Audio

GENERAL NON-FICTION

Eric Delderfield	**Eric Delderfield's Bumper Book of True Animal Stories**
Caroline Elliot	**The BBC Book of Royal Memories 1947-1990**
Joan Grant	**The Cuckoo on the Kettle**
Joan Grant	**The Owl on the Teapot**
Helene Hanff	**Letters From New York**
Martin Lloyd-Elliott	**City Ablaze**
Elizabeth Longford	**Royal Throne**
Joanna Lumley	**Forces Sweethearts**
Vera Lynn	**We'll Meet Again**
Desmond Morris	**The Animal Contract**
Anne Scott-James and Osbert Lancaster	**The Pleasure Garden**
Les Stocker	**The Hedgehog and Friends**
Elisabeth Svendsen	**Down Among the Donkeys**
Gloria Wood and Paul Thompson	**The Nineties**
The Lady Wardington	**Superhints for Gardeners**
Nicholas Witchell	**The Loch Ness Story**